D0975027

WHEN LIFE GIVES YOU DEMONS

Jennifer Honeybourn

Swoon READS

Swoon Reads • New York

A SWOON READS BOOK

An imprint of Feiwel and Friends and Macmillan Publishing Group, LLC
175 Fifth Avenue, New York, NY 10010

Our books may be purchased in bulk for promotional, educational, or business
use. Please contact your local bookseller or the Macmillan Corporate and
Premium Sales Department at (800) 221-7945 ext. 5442 or by e-mail at
MacmillanSpecialMarkets@macmillan.com.

Library of Congress Cataloging-in-Publication Data

Names: Honeybourn, Jennifer, author.
Title: When life gives you demons / Jennifer Honeybourn.
Description: First edition. | New York : Swoon Reads, 2018. | Summary:
    Shelby Black tries to juggle school, love, and her training, under her uncle's
    tutelage, to be an exorcist.
Identifiers: LCCN 2017041921 | ISBN 978-1-250-15823-9 (hardcover) |
    ISBN 978-1-250-15822-2 (ebook)
Subjects: | CYAC: Demonology—Fiction. | Exorcism—Fiction. | High
    schools—Fiction. | Schools—Fiction. | Uncles—Fiction. | Supernatural—
    Fiction. | Humorous stories.
Classification: LCC PZ7.1.H654 Whe 2018 | DDC [Fic]—dc23
LC record available at https://lccn.loc.gov/2017041921

Book design by Liz Dresner

First edition, 2018

10 9 8 7 6 5 4 3 2 1

swoonreads.com

For my friend Jennifer McKenzie

Chapter

1

"SHELBY, CONCENTRATE." Uncle Roy's eyebrows snap together, forcing the skin at the bridge of his nose into a deep wrinkle.

I sigh and hold the heavy silver crucifix a little bit higher. Mrs. Collins is chained to the bed, her thin arms stretched across the mattress and secured to the headboard with iron handcuffs. Sounds totally sadistic, but it's actually a necessary safety precaution. That old lady may look frail, but if she weren't restrained she could easily tear me apart. And from the way she's glaring at me with her crazy red demon eyes, I have no doubt she'd like to.

Before she was possessed, Mrs. Collins probably spent her days baking cookies for her grandchildren and planting tulips in her garden. Now? Her head is spinning on her neck like a globe on its axis, and she's using language that's so foul it makes my face burn.

Uncle Roy nudges me toward the bed. The crucifix starts to vibrate in my hands. Mrs. Collins's eyes widen and she strains against the handcuffs, her body arching toward the ceiling. She isn't wearing her false teeth, and her mouth is ghoulishly sunken in. Spit is flying everywhere, which is totally gross and part of the reason why I don't want to get too close to her. That and the kicking. Her legs are flying around like the blades of a windmill. She's working them so fast that her bottom starts to lift off the mattress, forcing her modest white nightgown to slide up to her hips in a very un-grandmotherly way and giving me a ringside view of her control-top underwear.

And then the rest of her starts to lift off the bed.

Crap. Looks like she's figured out how to levitate. I guess I should have pinned her legs down after all.

I sneak a look at Uncle Roy. He just sighs and shakes his head.

Lifting the crucifix up even higher, I close my eyes and start to mutter the incantation. "*Deus, in nómine tuo salvum me fac—*"

"Say it like you mean it," he says.

"*—et virtúte tua age causam meam—*"

"Louder!"

I glare at him. Seriously? How am I supposed to concentrate when he keeps interrupting?

"*Deus, audi oratiónem . . . meam . . . um . . . áuribus?*"

There's a reason why Latin is a dead language. It's impossible to learn. Which is why even though Uncle Roy has made me practice this chant a million times, I still struggle with it.

"*Áuribus pércipe . . .*" he prompts me.

"*Áuribus pércipe verba oris mei.*"

I make it through the rest of the incantation without stumbling. As I finish, I feel a shift in the air, and all the sound is suddenly sucked out of the room. Smiling, I open my eyes, expecting Mrs. Collins to be lying quietly against the pillows, returned to her sweet, seventy-year-old self, eternally grateful that I saved her soul.

Unfortunately, that is not what I see.

Mrs. Collins is still halfway in the air, twisting violently, her body being wrung out like a mop by some invisible force. Her tongue is swollen and hanging out of her mouth like a thick black eel, and her eyes . . . well, they've rolled completely back into her head.

So not only did the exorcism not work, but it seems to have agitated her even more.

Huh. Maybe I wasn't speaking loud enough. Or maybe if Uncle Roy just let me do this without butting in—

There's a splintering sound as Mrs. Collins suddenly yanks her arm back. Fortunately, it's just a piece of the headboard breaking and not her actual bones. She rolls onto her side, one of her hands now free, and tries to work the other handcuff off, so I begin the incantation again. But before I can even get the first few words out, Uncle Roy elbows me out of the way and stalks toward the bed, his black robe flapping behind him like a crow's wings.

"*Deus, audi oratiónem meam; áuribus pércipe verba oris mei,*" he bellows. "*Nam supérbi insurréxerunt contra me, et violénti quæsierunt vitam meam.*"

My jaw drops. I can't believe he's taking over. Again. I've been training three times a week for the past five months and he's still never let me finish an exorcism on my own.

Such a control freak.

With a huff, I collapse into an overstuffed floral armchair near the window. The lacy curtains are pulled shut so the neighbors won't see Mrs. Collins hovering over her bed like a UFO.

Uncle Roy continues the incantation, his voice strong and sure—the same way it sounds at the pulpit every Sunday. The kind of voice that even demons listen to.

Whatever. Who cares if I'm good at this or not? I'm not even sure I want to be an exorcist. He's the one pushing me to do it, insisting that I have a gift.

Some gift.

"*Nam ex omni tribulatióne eripuit me, et inimícos meos confúsos vidit óculos meus.*"

Mrs. Collins is still struggling to free herself, desperately chewing at her wrist like a wolf trying to escape a steel trap. As Uncle Roy reaches the end of the incantation, a blast of hot air causes his white hair to blow back—a definite sign that the demon is being wrenched out of Mrs. Collins. Sure enough, a few seconds later, she drops back down onto the bed, completely limp.

Uncle Roy doesn't lower his crucifix right away. Demons can be tricky. Sometimes they pretend they've gone and then, once your defenses are down, they attack. Just to make sure, he uncorks a small silver flask and sprinkles some holy water on her. It doesn't burn her skin—another good sign.

Mrs. Collins moans. Her eyes flutter open, and I can see that they've returned to their usual blue color. She stares at us, confused. The possessed generally have no recollection of what happened to them, and considering how most people behave while possessed, this is indeed a blessing.

Uncle Roy takes her hand—the one not handcuffed to the headboard—and gently strokes it. "It's all right, Rose. Just relax. You're going to be okay."

My irritation at him starts to fade a little; he has a very good bedside manner. That's one more thing, according to him, that I need to work on.

I get up and walk over to the bed. I pull Mrs. Collins's nightgown down over her legs and then unlock the handcuff holding her wrist. Her poor skin is raw from where she chewed at it. Good thing she didn't have her teeth in.

While Uncle Roy continues to comfort Mrs. Collins, I open the door and let her husband into the room. He's been pacing the hall for the past twenty minutes. Uncle Roy doesn't like family members to be present during an exorcism. They have a tendency to freak out when they see steam coming out of their loved one's ears.

Mr. Collins looks at me, his brown eyes hopeful. "Is she . . . ?"

I nod. "The demon's gone. She'll be fine."

His wrinkled old face crumples in relief. He rushes past me and kneels in front of Uncle Roy. He takes Uncle Roy's hand and kisses his gold signet ring as if Uncle Roy is the Godfather or something.

"Thank you, Father," Mr. Collins croaks.

Uncle Roy pats his shoulder. "Best to just let her rest tonight, Abe. I'll call you tomorrow to see how she's doing." He drops his silver flask into the black leather doctor's bag he uses to store his supplies and gestures for me to follow him.

We walk down the plastic runner path the Collinses have laid over their carpet and out the front door. As we climb into Uncle Roy's ancient green hatchback, I glance at the little brick house. From the outside, you'd never guess anything weird ever happened in there.

But then again, looks can be deceiving. I'm certainly proof of that.

Chapter

2

SPENCER CALLAGHAN rocks the hell out of a Catholic school uniform.

He's taken off his navy blazer and loosened his tie—the first thing he does as soon as the bell rings. His white shirt is still neatly tucked into the waistband of his gray flannel pants. The cuffs of his white dress shirt are turned up, revealing the antique silver watch he always wears with the face turned to the inside of his wrist.

"Hey," he says, watching me approach. He's leaning back in his chair, twirling a pencil in his fingers. His dark hair is rumpled and curling over his ears, longer than St. Joseph's High School would like it to be. It's this little assertion of independence—his refusal to conform by keeping his hair clipped really short—that first won me over.

"Hey." I drop into the seat beside him. This corner of the library, our usual meeting spot, is quiet and overlooks the school courtyard. Students are already starting to scatter, and in a matter of minutes, the courtyard will empty out. As soon as the bell rings, all anyone wants is to get as far away from the school as fast as possible, but this has become my favorite time of day, because it means I get alone time with Spencer.

"You want to start with geometry?" he says, leaning forward to open his textbook.

I wrinkle my nose. "Ugh. I hate geometry." I let my guidance counselor talk me into taking it after he quizzed me about my college plans and I mentioned I was interested in architecture. Unfortunately, architecture turned out to be only a passing interest, and now I'm stuck with this impossibly hard course.

"You may have mentioned that several hundred times," Spencer says.

"That's because I can't stress it enough."

He smiles and lightly taps the back of my hand with his pencil. He's not even touching me directly, and yet a thrill still runs all the way through me. "And that's why we should tackle it first," he says. "Eat the frog."

"Um . . . what?"

"It's an expression." He starts twirling his pencil again. "Mark Twain. Put the worst task behind you, and then you can get on with the rest of your day."

Where does he get this stuff?

"Well, it's definitely the worst task," I say, pulling my textbook out of my bag, careful not to let him see the big silver crucifix and bejeweled spray bottle of holy water that I have stashed inside. Because he would definitely have questions.

Spencer and I have been study buddies for the past few months, ever since shortly after he arrived at St. Joseph's, but I still don't feel like I know him all that well. He's pretty tight with details about his personal life. Then again, I don't share much about my life—it's not like I'm going to tell him I'm an exorcist. It's not exactly something I brag about. Even my best friend, Vanessa, doesn't know about my extracurricular activity.

Here's the thing: I go to a Catholic school. Most of the kids at St. Joseph's believe in heaven and hell, in God and Satan. If they found out that I have direct experience with evil spirits, they would probably publicly shun me. And while

I don't have many friends, I want to hang on to the ones I do have. Even if that means not ever letting them know who I really am.

We work silently, the only sound Spencer's pencil scratching across his paper.

"Hey, what'd you get for the first question?" I ask him a few minutes later, casually trying to sneak a glance at his homework.

He places his palm over his paper to hide the answer from me, but not before I see that he's already almost finished the entire page. He narrows his eyes. "First, tell me what you got."

"You're supposed to be helping me."

"Helping you study, not helping you cheat," he says.

"Cheating is pretty much the only way I'm going to pass this course." I put my head down on the table. I'm debating whether to just give up and gracefully accept that I'm destined to fail when Spencer does something totally unexpected; he reaches over and strokes my hair, light as a butterfly.

My breath catches. I don't want to move in case he stops. But I hear him shuffle his papers, and when I sit up, Spencer's eyes are already back on his homework. He's diligently focused on the last question, like whatever just happened didn't happen at all. He's so stone-faced that I begin to question whether I even felt anything, or if I just want him to make a move so bad that I'm imagining things.

I turn back to my own homework, wondering if I'll ever unravel the mystery that is Spencer Callaghan.

✖ ✖

Ever since my mom left, I've been in charge of the grocery shopping in our house—a task that Uncle Roy has tried to take back several times in the past five months, because he isn't thrilled with what I bring home: heavy on the fruits and vegetables, very little sugar, zero foods that contain ingredients that aren't found in nature. What he doesn't seem to understand is that he's the reason I buy that stuff in the first place. The fact is, he's old, and I'm determined to keep him healthy. Pumping him full of kale smoothies and quinoa will hopefully help him live to be a hundred.

I'm not nearly as strict with my own diet. I have dinner at Vanessa's house at least twice a week, where I eat my fill of meatloaf and mashed potatoes drowning in butter or tuna casserole with saltine crackers crumbled on top.

"Shelby, honey, grab me some oregano, would you?" Mrs. O'Malley says as I walk in the back door. She's standing in front of the stove, stirring a huge pot of red sauce, a tea towel featuring a cartoon lobster hanging over one shoulder. The kitchen is as steamy as a sauna and smells like garlic and tomatoes.

I root through the spice rack for the oregano and pass it

to her. Mrs. O'Malley twists off the cap and turns the glass bottle over, sending a shower of dried green flakes into the sauce.

"Before you run off . . ." she begins, setting the bottle on the counter. Her glasses are all steamed up. When she slips them off and wipes the lenses on the tea towel, I notice the bags underneath her eyes. I guess that's to be expected when you have four kids. "How are things going? Are you doing okay?"

What she's really asking is how I'm doing without my mom. I've told everyone that she's on an extended trip to Italy to visit relatives. It's not like I can tell them the truth: that my mom's actually training at some supersecret exorcism school in Rome. It wouldn't be so bad if she'd at least said good-bye. We'd had a big fight, so I'd told her that I was sleeping at Vanessa's. When I got home the next morning, she was gone. She didn't even tell me she was leaving. She let Uncle Roy break the news to me. Thinking about it now, hurt rushes through me.

I can tell from the way Mrs. O'Malley's mouth turns down whenever she mentions my mother that she thinks she's awful for leaving me. I can't imagine what she'd say if she knew that I haven't heard from her since she left.

Not a phone call, not an e-mail.

Nothing.

She's still angry with me, and I can't exactly blame her. I said some awful things—things I didn't mean—and even though Uncle Roy claims that the reason we haven't heard from her is because the school discourages outside contact, I know the truth.

"I'm all right." I think I sound pretty convincing until Mrs. O'Malley leans over and gives me a hug. She's like an octopus, squeezing me so hard that I have trouble breathing, but I let her do it. I maybe even hug her back.

"I'm sure Robin will be back soon," she says when she finally releases me. She doesn't sound confident, though, and it occurs to me that maybe Mrs. O'Malley doesn't think my mom is ever coming back. In my darkest moments, the thought has crossed my mind, but I just can't believe that my mom would actually abandon me forever, no matter how mad she is at me.

I nod.

"You need anything, you just let me know, okay?" Mrs. O'Malley says.

"Thanks."

I'm halfway up the stairs when I hear Vanessa and her sister fighting. Before I reach the door, Izzy comes streaking out of their room, her face contorted with fury. She darts past me on the stairs, hollering for her mother.

"We have about thirty seconds before Hurricane Sharon

comes storming up here," Vanessa says. She's sitting on her bed, calmly flipping through a copy of *Teen Vogue* with an "Isabelle" label tacked on the front cover.

"So? How'd it go with Spencer?" She rolls up the magazine and holds it up to her eye like a telescope, pretending to focus so she can see me better.

"You know Iz is going to kill you when she sees what you've done to her magazine," I say.

"Maybe it will teach her to stay out of my closet." Vanessa unspools the magazine. The pages are curled beyond repair. She tosses it onto Izzy's bed and lies back against her pillow, her dark hair wild around her head. "Having to share a room with an uptight thirteen-year-old is my own personal hell." She sighs. "Now stop trying to change the subject. Spencer. Details."

I sit down at the end of her bed. I think about telling her how he stroked my hair so we can analyze what it means, but I already know that Vanessa will proclaim it's a sign that he likes me. I don't want my heart to be convinced that it's true when he might not have meant anything by it.

"Nothing to report."

She shakes her head. "Just make a move already. Quit being such a chicken," she says, nudging me with her foot.

Chicken? She wouldn't say that if she could see me facing down a demon. Of course, she doesn't know that I'm an exorcist. Although, I'm sure that at some point she'll put two and two together. She'll remember the time she caught me filling up my flask with holy water from the fancy marble fountain in the church. Or when she noticed the weird burn marks on my leg—an injury from a particularly grueling exorcism. And once she discovers the truth . . . I don't know. I'd like to believe that Vanessa would still be my friend, but people can get weird about things like casting out demons. Even best friends.

"Vanessa!" Mrs. O'Malley bellows from the bottom of the stairs. "Get down here. Right. Now."

Vanessa makes a face. "Only one more year until I'm up for parole," she says, getting off the bed. "I swear, my main criterion for college is that it's in another state."

She stomps out of the room. Vanessa may think that being away from her family is the key to freedom, but she only has to look in my direction to know that freedom's not all it's cracked up to be. Even though I'm pretty good at covering it up, I miss my mom so much, it's a physical ache. It's a feeling that's always with me, as strong and solid as my heartbeat. Nothing will feel right until she's back and I can apologize. And the worst part is that I have no clue when that will be.

Chapter

3

UNCLE ROY glances at me over his half-moon glasses as I enter the rectory.

We usually complete the paperwork for an exorcism right away, but Uncle Roy was too tired to work on Mrs. Collins's file the other day. An exorcism can take a lot of energy, and I've noticed that they've affected him more than usual lately.

Maybe if he'd just let me do one myself, then he wouldn't be so tired.

I plunk down at the scarred wooden desk across from him. Moo, my cat, immediately settles across my feet. I grab a yellow legal pad and a pen from the ugly clay holder that one of the parishioners gave Uncle Roy for Christmas one year.

Uncle Roy says it's important to keep records. I get that, but I wish he would at least let me use a computer. He makes me handwrite everything because he's paranoid that someone will hack our files. I'm not sure who he thinks would care enough to do that—and what they'd do with the information if they did manage to get their hands on it—but when I complain, he lectures me about confidentiality. Going to see an exorcist? Not exactly something anyone wants made public.

Fair enough. I mean, it's definitely not something I want anyone to know I'm involved in. But I still wish I could use a computer.

"So, Shelby. What could you have done differently?" Uncle Roy taps a pencil against his lips.

"Uh . . . I don't know. Talk faster?" I reach down to move Moo off my feet; her weight has already made them fall asleep, sending prickles up my legs.

He nods. "Yes, but your pronunciation was off as well. And you were much too far from the bed! You need to get in there. Right up close."

"Within spitting distance? No thank you." I shudder.

Uncle Roy's eyes narrow. "Shelby, you need to take this seriously."

"I do take it seriously," I say, stamping my sleepy left foot against the threadbare Oriental carpet. "Maybe if you'd just let me finish one time—"

"You did finish," he interrupts. "And you failed."

I slouch in my chair, arms crossed. I can feel a headache coming on. Uncle Roy's lectures are worse than the paperwork.

"You need to practice the incantation," he says. "It's critical that you get it right. Do you know what can happen if you don't say it properly?"

"I know, I know. The exorcism won't work."

"True, but it's more than that." He sighs and tosses his pencil onto the desk. "These are very powerful words, Shelby. Say them wrong, and . . . well, you can compromise the very soul you're trying to save."

He's warned me about this before, of course. Many times. And it's not that I don't listen. It's just that, even after all my training, even after everything Uncle Roy has taught me, I'm still not convinced that I can actually do it—save someone's soul.

Most Catholics would argue that it's not possible. For one thing, I'm not a priest; exorcists are always priests, at least in the Catholic faith. Also, since there are no female priests, that also means there are no female exorcists by default. I'm zero for two.

Uncle Roy is a bit bendy on those particular rules.

"It's very important that you practice the incantation until you can say it in your sleep," he says.

I roll my eyes. As previously mentioned, Latin is a bitch to learn, so I feel like he should cut me some slack. I open my mouth to tell him that, but he holds up his hand to stop me.

"It's not just that you got the incantation wrong, Shelby. You also forgot to secure the legs." Uncle Roy scowls. "You could have been seriously hurt. Always secure the legs!" He bangs his fist on the desk for emphasis.

As he continues to nitpick my session, I stare over his shoulder at the painting of Mary hanging behind him on the wall. The painting is a bit Mona Lisa–like in that wherever I am in the room, her eyes seem to follow me. Its placement allows me to tune Uncle Roy out without him noticing that I'm not actually paying attention to him. Very handy.

Eventually Uncle Roy's lecture winds down, and he lets me get back to writing my report. With a sigh, I pick up my pen again and start to scribble.

Case Number: EX100-17-3792
Incident: The Exorcism of Rose Collins
Exorcist: Shelby Black

*At approximately 1600 hours on the
2nd of May, Father Roy and I met
with Abe Collins regarding his wife,
Rose Collins. Mr. Collins believed that
his wife was presenting signs of demonic
possession—suffering from nightmares,
talking in tongues, sharp decline in
personal hygiene, etc.*

*After consulting with Mr. Collins—
a longtime parishioner of St. Jude's—
Father Roy and I agreed to visit his wife
the next—*

Moo suddenly leaps on top of the desk, sending the pages of my report flying. Uncle Roy quickly pushes his chair back as far as possible. My cat has been in the room with us for the past twenty minutes, hidden near my feet, but Uncle Roy only ever sneezes when he actually sees her.

"Shoo," he says, flapping his hands at her. "Shoo!"

Moo stays right where she is, staring him down, daring him to touch her. I fight a smile. She knows that Uncle Roy is "allergic" to her; she just likes to screw with him.

Moo is a stray. She's white with wide green eyes. She looks innocent, but she's a scrapper. The tip of her ear is missing from some long-ago cat fight. She showed up on our doorstep one night last year, and, after much begging, Uncle Roy let me keep her. I guess he must have a soft spot for strays. After all, he took me and Mom in after Dad left to "find himself" in California. Staying with Uncle Roy was supposed to be short-term, just until we got back on our feet. But two years later, we're still here. Or I am, anyway.

Uncle Roy sneezes. I grab Moo off of the table and give her a scratch behind the ears before setting her in the hall and kicking the door closed with the toe of my sneaker.

I sit back down at my desk. As he continues to snuffle, I turn back to my report.

> . . . day. When we arrived, Father Roy asked **me** to lead the exorcism. He stayed out in the hall while I conducted a survey of the scene. Mrs. Collins was in her room, still in bed, although not asleep. The room totally reeked like sulfur, so I was confident that possession had occurred.
>
> I quickly handcuffed a half-asleep Mrs. Collins to the bed. Being that she

*was so old, I didn't think it was
necessary to chain her legs as well,
although, according to some people, I
should have.*

The sun has begun its descent behind the mountains, and the office is quickly getting dark. Uncle Roy leans over and flicks on his faux Tiffany desk lamp. Colored light spills across my page.

*Once I had her secured, Father Roy
came into the room to **supervise**. When
she saw him, Mrs. Collins totally
freaked and started struggling to get
free. Typical reaction, as demons aren't
too fond of priests.*

*I started the incantation. I forgot one
word, which does not seem like such a
big deal to me, especially considering
that this was supposed to be my first
time doing an exorcism on my own.
Unfortunately, when I finished the
chant, Mrs. Collins was still possessed.
This could be due to a number of*

*reasons, but I think it's mainly because Father Roy kept interrupting me. It's **very hard to concentrate** when someone keeps interrupting you.*

At that point, Father Roy jumped in— even though I was handling it—and completed the exorcism.

By the time I've finished the report, my hand is cramped and it's completely dark outside. It's been a long day, and my brain is foggy.

Uncle Roy peers over his glasses at me. "All done?"

I rip the pages off the legal pad and hand them over. He riffles through them, *tsk*ing at my terrible handwriting, then slides the report into a file folder, which he locks inside one of the steel filing cabinets lining the wall. He wears the key to the filing cabinets on a chain around his neck. I've never seen him take it off.

Like I said, he takes confidentiality very seriously.

"I'll see you back at the house," he says, turning back to his work.

I stand up and stretch. I grab my messenger bag from underneath the desk. I'm almost out the door when he says, "And, Shelby?"

I turn around, but Uncle Roy doesn't look up.

"Make sure you practice the incantation."

✗ ✗

I walk quickly past the small cemetery that lies between the church and our small clapboard house. All of the headstones are ancient—the cemetery ran out of room a long time ago—so it feels less creepy than if the epitaphs held the names of people I actually knew. Less creepy, but still creepy.

I zip up the steps of our house and through the screen door. Stopping in the kitchen, I grab a sleeve of graham crackers and a glass of milk, then head down the narrow hall toward the back of the house.

There's a new painting on the wall—a big blob of red with a black center. Uncle Roy is way into painting lately, and his rudimentary canvases are all over our house. He only paints flowers, for some reason, and I think this one is supposed to be a poppy. He's a terrible artist, and he doesn't seem to be improving, even though he's been painting for months. Part of me wonders if he enjoys it as much as he claims or if he's just sticking with it because he hates to quit anything.

I continue down the hall. The screened-in porch at the back of the house is probably my favorite place in the world. It faces a copse of evergreen trees, and when it rains, which it does a lot of in Seattle, I sit out here and listen to it drum against the roof.

After setting my milk and graham crackers on the rickety wooden crate we use for a side table, I reach underneath the chair's thick, orange cushion for my copy of *Rituale Romanum*—the official book of Catholic rituals. It's this incredibly old book that contains all of the Catholic rituals and rites—baptism, penance, marriage. Near the very end of the book, past everything else, is a fifty-eight-page section on exorcism.

Exorcism is all very underground. It's not like Uncle Roy advertises his services, but the people who need his help most always seem to find him anyway. Part of the reason why he's so adamant about training me is that, according to him, the universe is unbalanced. There are way more demons than there are people who know how to expel them.

I don't like to think about that too much.

I sink into the chair, the leather-bound book heavy on my lap. *Rituale Romanum* was originally published in the sixteen hundreds, but the rituals themselves go all the way back to the first century. The English-translated copy that I have is only about ten years old, though. It belonged to my mom. I found it in her room after she left for Italy.

I flip to the list of instructions. Twenty-one detailed directions on how to conduct an exorcism. I don't need to read them; I know them by heart. The sight of the notes my mom has made in the margins—her tiny, cramped printing—makes my throat tighten. I have cried over this book so many times that the ink on the pages has started to run.

All these months later, I still can't believe that she left without saying good-bye. She left and forgot about my existence as easily as my dad seemed to. And I know she was mad at me—we'd been fighting for weeks over really stupid stuff, like why it was always my job to unload the dishwasher, or why making dinner and cleaning the bathrooms was suddenly my responsibility, but I never expected her to drop out of my life.

I wish I could figure out what it is about me that makes me so easy to forget.

She'd seemed stressed for months—I think she was having trouble finding the balance between her job as a legal secretary and her exorcism work—and that made her snappier than usual. Instead of cutting her some slack and trying to understand what she was going through, I felt resentful. I was tired of always being at the bottom of her list and sick of the extra housework she kept heaping on me. After all, she wasn't the only one with responsibilities.

Uncle Roy knew we weren't getting along, of course. You couldn't live in our house and not feel the tension. But he wasn't home the night we had our biggest fight. He insists that it's a coincidence that my mom left for some exorcism school I'd never heard of the very same night we had that terrible argument, but he didn't hear the awful things I said to her. If he did, he wouldn't be on my side.

I've sent my mom a hundred e-mails since that night. I call her cell phone every day, but all I get is her voice mail. She remains as impossible to reach as the moon. So all I can do is hope that she cools off soon and comes home.

I really need her to come home.

Chapter

4

THE NEXT AFTERNOON, Vanessa and I walk past the boys' lacrosse team warming up on the grass field. This isn't our normal route home from school—we have to go out of our way to walk past the field—but Spencer is on the team, and I will take every chance I can get to see him in shorts.

I spot him right away, standing on the sidelines beside Coach Lee. Spencer's wearing the team uniform, a navy-blue jersey with the number seventeen on the back and baggy blue shorts, but he's not suited up in pads like the rest of the team.

"Spencer!" Vanessa calls, waving like a maniac and making a complete spectacle of herself. And, by association, of me.

"What are you doing?" I grab her hand and hold it down, even though it's way too late because *oh my God* he's already seen us. I feel my cheeks start to heat up. I was hoping to quietly admire Spencer from afar—I don't want him to think that I deliberately came by to see him. Even though I did.

Vanessa rolls her eyes. "I'm trying to help move this along," she says. "That boy is hot. You'd better get on it, Shelby, because the wolves are circling. Bex Wagner was all up in his personal space in bio yesterday."

My stomach sinks. I could almost handle it if Vanessa had named any other senior girl, but, ugh, Bex Wagner is the worst. She is gorgeous, no debate, but she has a heinous personality. She's the girl most likely to take your boyfriend. And she does. Frequently.

Vanessa is probably telling me this to force my hand. She knows how I feel about Bex. And I think my all-talk/no-action approach when it comes to Spencer is starting to drive her crazy.

Spencer says something to Coach Lee and then heads toward us. His dark hair is all messy, exactly the way I like it. As he closes the distance between us, I can see that he's smiling, and my insides get all melty. If he only knew the power that smile holds over me. . . .

"You're not playing?" Vanessa asks him when he's finally standing in front of us.

He shakes his head. "Sitting this one out. I did something to my leg during practice yesterday."

He's not playing, but he's still here supporting his team? God, I love him.

"What are you two up to?" he asks.

"Just on the way home," I say. I have training in twenty minutes, and if I don't hustle, I'm going to be late. And Uncle Roy isn't a fan of lateness. I've learned that the hard way. One time, he made me write out the entire incantation in long-hand twenty times all because I was five minutes late. Five minutes!

Spencer's phone buzzes. He pulls it out of his pocket. Whatever he sees on the screen makes him tense up. He glances around the field, at his teammates gathered in a circle, the handful of people who have showed up to watch the game, the woman on the other side of the field digging in the recycling bin. My stomach tightens. I hope he's not looking for Bex Wagner.

Vanessa elbows me. I know she wants me to say something, anything, that will show him I'm interested so he doesn't ride off into the sunset with Bex, but I can't seem to get any words out. My mouth is dry. I'm not usually tongue-tied around Spencer, but the sight of him in his lacrosse uniform is scrambling my brain.

The whistle blows. Frowning, he slides his phone back into his pocket. "I'd better get back," he says. He reaches out and touches my arm. "See you tomorrow?"

I nod. We have a study session every Wednesday after school. Wednesdays have become my favorite day of the week. I live for Wednesdays.

"He touched your arm!" Vanessa says when Spencer's barely out of earshot. "He didn't touch Bex once in bio, and, trust me, with the way she was draped over him, that couldn't have been easy."

I'm not loving the mental image of Bex and her blond perfection all over Spencer, but it has to mean something that he resisted her charms. He's probably the only boy that has ever managed to.

As I watch Spencer walk back to join his teammates, I decide that Vanessa is right—I need to do something about Spencer Callaghan.

✕ ✕

". . . *inimícos meos confuses vidit óculos meus.*" I can't keep the smile off my face. I made it through the entire incantation with no prompting! There is no way Uncle Roy can find fault. For once, he has absolutely nothing to criticize.

I hold my hand out, waiting for him to slap my palm. But he just leans back in his chair, crosses his arms, and says, "Again."

Seriously? I've recited the incantation ten times in the past hour. I've also spent two hours practicing my handcuffing technique. Uncle Roy may be seventy years old, but he's very strong. He fights as hard as any demon.

"But I just did it perfectly!"

He shrugs. "Then you should have no trouble doing it perfectly again."

Fine. He wants to hear the incantation again? I'll do it again.

"*Deus . . . in . . . nómine . . . tuo . . . salvum . . .* " I speak as slowly as possible. In a bad Cockney accent.

Uncle Roy sighs, exasperated. "Shelby, if you're not going to take this seriously, then we can—"

He's interrupted by a knock on the door. A tiny, owlish-looking woman pokes her head into the office. "Father Roy?"

"Mrs. Harris, come in. We've been expecting you."

We have?

"Come in, come in." He waves her inside.

Mrs. Harris crosses the carpet and settles into the armchair across from Uncle Roy's desk, clutching her black patent-leather purse to her chest. Her dark hair is pulled back with a wide red headband, and she's wearing a floral dress that is really doing nothing for her.

"You wanted to speak to me about your son, Shane? You believe he's under an evil influence?" Uncle Roy asks.

"Um . . . well, yes, but . . ." Mrs. Harris glances at me. "Maybe it would be best if we spoke in private. I don't want anyone to know about my son's . . . problem."

"No need to worry about Shelby," he says. "She's my apprentice. There's nothing she hasn't heard before."

I give Mrs. Harris a reassuring smile, but she does not seem to be reassured.

"It's not something I want getting around the school," she says, giving me the once-over.

Wait, what? Just because I'm a teenager, she assumes I'm not a professional? That I can't keep a secret?

Rude.

"Lydia, I assure you, your case will be kept completely confidential," Uncle Roy says. "I trust Shelby implicitly."

Mrs. Harris takes a minute to consider this before giving him a curt nod. I guess she figures she can't argue with a priest. Not when she needs his help.

"So." Uncle Roy uncaps his fountain pen. "What makes you think your son is possessed?"

The word makes Mrs. Harris flinch. "He's not himself

lately. He never leaves his bedroom. He's up all night playing violent video games, and when he does come out, he won't talk to me." She lowers her eyes and fiddles with the clasp on her purse. "He's belligerent and rude. The language he uses is just awful. He only wears black. And his eyes . . ."

Uncle Roy looks up from his yellow legal pad. "What about them?"

"They're very red. I've tried to get him to see an optometrist, but he insists it's just allergies." She shakes her head. "I have allergies. My eyes never look like that."

"Tell me, have you noticed a particular smell?" he asks her.

"Now that you mention it, yes," she says, sitting up straighter. "He does sort of smell."

Is she for real? Her son isn't possessed—he's a teenager. One who likes to get stoned, I'll bet. I steal a glance at Uncle Roy. He shakes his head slightly, warning me to keep quiet.

"What about his voice? Any changes?"

"It's deeper. And sort of . . . growly."

I wait for Uncle Roy to tell her about puberty, but instead he just nods thoughtfully. "When did this all start?"

"Well, he's been quite depressed since we moved here a few months ago, so at first I thought that's all it was. I thought he was just adjusting to his new life," she says. "But in the last few weeks things have gotten worse. And then last Sunday . . ." Her eyes fill with tears. She grabs a wad of tissues out of the box Uncle Roy keeps on his desk.

"He wouldn't come with me to church. He says he'll never set foot in church again." She dabs at her eyes. "He used to be an altar boy."

Uncle Roy puts the cap back on his pen. "I think we should take a look at him. Shelby, would you mind paying a visit to Shane?"

I narrow my eyes at him, but he just smiles. He knows as well as I do that Mrs. Harris's son isn't possessed. What I can't figure out is why he's not telling her that.

Mrs. Harris is alarmed. "Father, I don't mean to be disrespectful, but are you sure . . . ?" She glances at me, frowning. "I mean, she's so young."

This is the point where I should jump in and tell her that this is all just a big waste of time. But it really bugs me that she doesn't think I can do it, so I don't bother telling her that there's nothing wrong with her son.

"Shelby is perfectly qualified to help Shane, Mrs. Harris. I wouldn't send her if I didn't think she was capable of getting to the bottom of this. Please don't worry," he says. "If she runs into any trouble, she knows she can call me and I'll come right over."

The only trouble I'm going to have is convincing Shane

to drop the attitude. My crucifix and holy water won't work on that.

"Well, if you're sure," Mrs. Harris says reluctantly.

"I couldn't be more sure," he says. "Now, how does tomorrow afternoon after school sound?"

Her face sags with relief. "That's perfect. Thank you, Father."

I wait until the door closes behind her before rounding on Uncle Roy. "Why are you making me do this?"

He rips the page off his legal pad and hands it to me. He's written the Harris's address at the top. "Just because her son isn't possessed doesn't mean he doesn't have a problem, Shelby," he says. "We help people. That's the job."

"I thought the job was getting rid of demons."

He shrugs. "Who says Shane doesn't have demons?" he says, settling back into his chair. "Now, I believe you were going to do the incantation one more time."

Chapter

5

SPENCER IS waiting at my locker after school. Unfortunately, I can't study with him today because I have an appointment.

With the devil.

Okay, not really. But paying a friendly visit to Mrs. Harris's son instead of spending time with Spencer certainly feels like hell. Uncle Roy has no idea what I'm giving up in order to do this.

"Sorry, I meant to text you," I say, opening my locker and grabbing my messenger bag. The truth is, I didn't forget to text him. I just wanted to see him, even if it was only for a few minutes. "Tomorrow?"

"You do know we have a geometry test in first period tomorrow, right?" he says, frowning. "And you also know you can't afford to fail this test."

"I'm not going to fail," I say. There's always a chance I'll scrape by. My grades have suffered ever since my mom left, which is why I was so happy when Spencer offered to tutor me a couple months ago. Not only because he's helping me get my grade point average up, but also because I'd been crushing on him for weeks and I didn't think he even knew my name.

But even at the risk of failing geometry, there's no way I'm going to flake out on Mrs. Harris this afternoon and prove to her that a teenager can't handle an exorcism. Even a fake exorcism.

"I have something I need to take care of that just can't wait. It's important." I slide my bag over my shoulder and close my locker door.

"More important than thirty percent of your grade?" he says.

"Definitely not. But I have to do it anyway."

He sighs, exasperated, but he's fighting a smile. "All right, what about later tonight? I'm running a study session in the library."

"It's a date," I say. As soon as the words are out of my mouth, my face starts to burn. Following our afterschool study sessions, Spencer runs study sessions every Wednesday evening for St. Joseph's underperforming students. I know this, and yet I said "date" anyway. I've basically just declared my feelings for him right to his face.

His smile widens, and the tips of his ears turn red. I'm not sure how to read his response—is it a good sign, one that means he's embarrassed because he likes me, too? Or is it a bad sign because he's embarrassed for me?

"Um, I should get going," I say. "See you tonight."

✕ ✕

Parking near the Harris's house is nothing short of a nightmare. By the time I finally wedge Uncle Roy's Honda between two SUVs and jog the half mile to their front door, I'm sweaty and aggravated and twenty minutes late. And in no mood to spend the afternoon trying to convince some spoiled kid to be nicer to his mother.

I speed-walk up the driveway. The curtains twitch, and a second later Mrs. Harris opens the door, making a point to frown at her watch. For someone who's expecting me to chase the evil spirits out of her son, she doesn't seem particularly grateful. I'd turn around and leave if I didn't think that Uncle Roy would just make me come right back.

"Couldn't find parking," I say.

Mrs. Harris gives me a tight smile but doesn't move to let me inside. I can't figure out why she's blocking the door, so we just stare at each other until finally she cracks and asks me to remove my shoes.

Whatever. I'm not about to argue with her, I just want to get this whole thing over with, so I kick off my loafers, hoping she doesn't notice the quarter-size hole in the toe of my tights.

You can tell a lot about a person by their house. The Harris's place is very formal—all overstuffed chairs, heavy swag curtains, and ballerina figurines that probably cost more than Uncle Roy's car. And it's obsessively clean. Like vacuum-tracks-in-the-carpet clean.

No wonder her son won't come out of his room. This whole place screams "don't touch anything." Definitely not somewhere a fourteen-year-old boy would hang out.

Mrs. Harris leads me down the hall, past a wide picture window with a distant view of the Space Needle. She stops in front of a white door with a glow-in-the-dark skull and crossbones sticker crookedly pasted on it.

"He went right in after school," she says, rapping her knuckles against the wood.

No answer.

"Shane, honey? There's someone here to see you. A friend." Mrs. Harris twists the brass knob, but, of course, the door is locked. She gives me a *see what I have to deal with?* look before withdrawing a silver letter opener from her dress pocket. When she slides it into the keyhole, the door pops open.

The first thing that hits me is the smell.

Demons usually give off a disgusting rotten-egg odor. Smell alone isn't a foolproof way to diagnose demonic possession, though, especially in a room that belongs to a teenage boy. Kind of hard to know whether there's an actual demon presence or if someone just had one too many bean burritos for lunch.

I'm guessing in this case that it's the latter. Mostly because of the mounds of fast-food wrappers littered everywhere, but also because I can tell, just by the way Shane's eyes are glued to his computer, that he's not possessed. Demons tend to be more interested in wreaking havoc and spreading evil in real life than in computer games.

Shane's so engrossed in whatever end-of-the-world game he's playing that he doesn't notice we've entered his lair. The volume on his headphones is turned up so loud that I can hear the rapid-fire sound of his virtual machine gun.

"Shane, honey? This is Shelby."

When Shane honey doesn't answer, Mrs. Harris marches over and shakes his shoulder. He stiffens, then yanks off his headphones and spins around in his black leather gaming chair with the built-in joysticks.

"What the hell, Mom?" he says. "I just about had him! You ruined my mission. Thanks a lot. Do you know how long it took me to—" He glances at me through the limp strands of his dyed-black hair. "Who are you?"

"I'll take it from here, Mrs. Harris," I say.

Mrs. Harris's eyes dart nervously to her son. He gives her such an evil glare that I can see why she thinks he's possessed. "Are you sure . . . ?"

I nod. "We'll be okay."

She leaves, and I push the door shut behind her.

Shane crosses his arms. "What's going on? Who are you?"

"I'm Shelby. I'm here because your mom's worried about you. She says you've been acting weird, and she thought it would help if you talked to someone."

He snorts. "So you're, like, what? Some kind of teen counselor or something?"

"Or something." I start to set my messenger bag down on his unmade bed, but then think better of it. God knows when he last washed those sheets.

"I don't need to talk to anyone. What I need is to be left alone," he says.

"Really? I guess if all you want from your freshman year is a high score on some stupid alien game, then—"

"Demons, not aliens," he mumbles. "I'm killing demons."

Oh, *come on*. . . .

"Step aside." I hang my bag on the back of Shane's chair before nudging him out of the seat. I sink into the soft, damp indent made by his butt—*blech!*—and wrap my hand around the joystick.

And then I kick some serious demon ass.

"Are you sure you've never played this before?" Shane asks, awestruck, once I've handed a few of the dark spirits a one-way ticket back to hell.

"Nope." At least, not on a computer. Okay, not in real life, either, but my training has to count for something.

After I've killed the last demon and earned Shane's respect, I swivel around to face him. He's staring at me like I'm Lara Croft or something.

I roll the chair back a few inches to put a bit more space between us. "So are you going to tell me what's going on with you?"

He flops onto his bed, stares up at the ceiling. "I don't know. It's just . . . my mom drives me crazy. She's always hovering. You know?"

I don't, actually. My mom hasn't hovered over me in

months. Because she can't. Because she's a million miles away in Italy.

"Maybe she would back off a bit if you came out of your cave and talked to her sometimes," I say. "She's lonely."

Shane's face darkens. "She wouldn't be lonely if she'd stayed with my dad."

And there it is. The real reason he's so angry.

"She left him?"

"She thinks he drinks too much. She didn't even give him the chance to try and change; we just left," he says. "She didn't ask me how I felt about it. Now I'm stuck in a new school and I hate it. Literally everyone at St. Joseph's sucks."

"Aw, come on. St. Joseph's isn't so bad," I say. "Give it a chance."

He rolls his eyes. "Right. Like everyone has given me a chance."

Shane's weird, there's no getting around it, but he could obviously use a friend. It occurs to me that maybe this is why Uncle Roy wanted me to come over here. I know what it's like to feel alone—I've certainly felt that way a lot, especially since my mom left—and if all it takes to help Shane is to be his friend, then I can do that.

"I'll introduce you to some people," I say. "And I'll even come by and kick your ass at *Demon Souls* again."

A shadow of a smile crosses Shane's face. "Promise?"

"Promise," I say, smiling back at him. "Now do your mom a favor and clean up your room." I glance around at the mess and shudder. "Seriously, you're going to single-handedly bring back the black plague."

He blushes. "I guess I can do that."

I stand up and grab my bag from the back of the chair. "I have to get going. But come find me tomorrow at school, okay?"

Shane nods.

I'm about to pull the door open when he says, "Shelby?"

I turn around.

"Thanks."

"No problem."

As soon as I'm in the hall, Mrs. Harris hustles toward me.

"Demon's gone," I say. "He'll be fine. Just make sure he drinks lots of water."

Mrs. Harris is so happy she actually hugs me.

Maybe I'm better at this bedside manner thing than I thought.

Chapter

6

EVERYONE IN the study group has already left by the time I get to the library. Everyone except Spencer.

"Sorry I'm so late," I say. Uncle Roy made me write the report on Shane's "exorcism" before he'd let me leave the house. I'm still not clear on why I had to document something that didn't even happen, but I know better than to argue with Uncle Roy about paperwork. That stupid report set me back almost an hour. When I told him that he'd probably just cost me a passing grade in geometry, Uncle Roy countered by pointing out that if my entire grade rested on the outcome of one test, then perhaps I should dedicate the afternoons when I'm not training to studying instead of "gallivanting around."

I pretty much have zero afternoons off from training—and no time for fun, ever—and he knows it, so I'm not sure how he could even say that to me with a straight face. But somehow he managed it.

I sit down beside Spencer. "Thanks for sticking around."

"Not a problem," he says, giving me a smile. He's still wearing his uniform, even though it's after six o'clock, which means he's been here since the bell rang. I bounce a little in my seat. This proves he likes me. Why else would he wait around after all the other students left?

Then Spencer hands me a sheet of practice questions and my happiness dims a little. Two months of studying and geometry still looks like hieroglyphics to me.

I sag in my chair. "There's no way I'm going to pass this test."

"You can, and you will," he replies as his phone starts to buzz. He picks it up and glances at the screen. From the storm cloud that drifts across his face, it's clear that whoever is on the other end is not someone he wants to hear from.

He ignores the call and sets his phone back on the table,

but it starts to vibrate again almost immediately. Whoever it is isn't taking no for an answer.

Spencer sighs. "Sorry," he says, pushing his chair back. "I have to take this." He stands up and stalks off to the other end of the library, so there's no chance I can overhear his conversation. This leaves me to assume that the reason he isn't taking the call in front of me is because he doesn't want me to know who he's talking to.

My stomach plunges. He has a girlfriend. It's the only explanation. Of course, he hasn't mentioned a girlfriend, but I have nothing but the sketchiest details about Spencer's personal life. I haven't been able to find him on social media, so all I really know about him is what he's told me, which is that he has an older brother and his parents are sociology professors and that they moved to Seattle from Portland a few months ago.

I can't even be upset with him if he does have a girlfriend, because it's not like he's led me on. And what's worse than liking someone who doesn't like you back?

Nothing, that's what.

I try to focus on the practice questions, but I'm way too distracted by Spencer to concentrate.

I glance over at him. His face is stony. I know that expression—it's the same one I get when Uncle Roy is giving me an earful. Spencer must feel my eyes on him, because his gaze flicks to me. Something that looks a lot like guilt crosses his features.

That settles it. He's got a girlfriend. Why else would he look so guilty?

I press my pencil down so hard onto the paper that the lead snaps. I'm busy digging in my bag for a sharpener when Spencer walks back over and settles into the seat beside me. He's sitting closer than he was before, close enough that I can smell his peppermint shampoo. "How's it coming?" he asks.

"It's not." I sigh and hold up my broken pencil. "Maybe it's a sign. The geometry gods are telling me to give up."

"I know you're frustrated, but you'll get it," he says. "I know you will."

His arm accidentally brushes against mine. Only maybe it's not an accident, because he's not moving away. His shirt is rolled up just beneath his elbows, so his bare arm is touching my bare arm—*our naked skin is touching*—and he is not moving away.

"Well, that makes one of us," I say. "So was that your girlfriend?"

Supersubtle.

I pretend to be really into sharpening my pencil so that I don't have to look at him while he breaks my heart.

"No. I don't have a girlfriend," he says. I can hear the smile in his voice. "That was my friend Lucas."

I bite my lip to keep from smiling back, but my cheeks are burning up, so hello, dead giveaway. If he didn't realize I had a thing for him before now, then my face has pretty much just advertised it for me.

And then Spencer asks, "What about you? Are you seeing anyone?" and maybe he's just making casual conversation, and I know I probably put too much faith in signs, but his knee is now touching mine, and holy hell, the fireworks.

I shake my head because I don't trust myself to speak.

He doesn't move his leg, not for the next forty minutes while we work through the practice questions. It's distracting, for sure, but I try to pay attention. But it's hard because I hate geometry, and also, our legs are touching! I am trying to keep my heart from jumping out of my chest, but Spencer is so laser-focused on helping me pass this test that he doesn't seem to notice. He just keeps on working, pencil scratching against paper, like the air between us isn't charged.

Somehow I make it through the practice questions. Geometry and I will probably never be friends, but by the time Mrs. Radcliff kicks us out of the library, I feel like I might just scrape by tomorrow.

Spencer clears his throat. "You need a ride home?" he asks as we gather up our books.

My stomach flips. He's never offered to drive me home before. This, right here, is our relationship going to the next level.

"That would be great," I say.

Neither of us says anything as we walk through the empty school. I'd like to say it's a companionable silence, but it's totally fraught with tension, at least on my end. I'm pretty sure Spencer feels it, too. He keeps clearing his throat like he's going to say something, but nothing comes out. Also, he keeps jingling his keys.

The weather has taken a turn. The rain is pelting down so hard that we have to run to his car, an old black VW Beetle. His car is on the far end of the student parking lot, which is just far enough to guarantee that we're both soaked by the time we reach it. Spencer opens the passenger door first, reaching in to chuck a bulky black lacrosse bag into the back seat.

While I climb in, he races around to the driver's side. He wipes his sleeve across his forehead. His dark hair is plastered to his face. I didn't bother to bring a jacket—didn't think I'd need one—so I cross my arms over my chest. I know from experience that the white collared shirt that I have to wear as part of my Catholic school uniform is pretty much transparent when it's wet.

Spencer starts the car. I'm shivering, so he fiddles with the air vents, aiming them in my direction. "It takes awhile for the heat to come on," he says. "One of the drawbacks of having a really old car."

"Hey, at least you have a car." I'm stuck driving Uncle Roy's Honda when I can convince him to lend it to me, which is not often. He prefers that I walk everywhere, claiming it's good for me, but really, I think it's just payback for weaning him off of sugar.

"You live on Maple, right? Behind St. Jude's?" he asks, pulling out of the parking lot. "With your uncle?"

I glance at him, surprised. Spencer and his family go to a different church, so I didn't expect him to know where I live, much less that he'd know about Uncle Roy. But I guess this isn't too surprising; Uncle Roy has been around for centuries. Also, he's six foot four and wears his cassock pretty much everywhere—he doesn't exactly blend in with the woodwork.

"What's it like? Living with a priest?" Spencer asks.

This isn't the first time I've been asked this question. Vanessa has grilled me on this very subject many times. If she ever came over to my house, she'd see firsthand that

Uncle Roy's not as stern as he comes across at the pulpit every Sunday. I'm not saying he has the best sense of humor, but I have seen him crack a smile on occasion. But Vanessa is so intimidated by Uncle Roy that we mostly hang out at her place.

I lean toward the vent. The heat is finally working. "It's fine," I say. "I mean, it's not like he goes around preaching all the time." Well, not about God, anyway. Mostly he lectures me on leaving my wet towel hanging over the shower rod or not loading the dishwasher properly.

Spencer stops at a light. It's like he read my mind, because he says, "I heard your mom is in Italy."

Wow, he's really done his research. I don't even know how he knows this, because I haven't told that many people. But my mom is off-limits—not something I want to talk about with anyone. Even Spencer. So, okay, maybe he's not the only one who's closed off.

"Yeah, she's visiting family," I say, feeling a pinch of guilt at the lie.

I guess he can sense that I'm uncomfortable, because he doesn't ask any more questions. I shift in my seat. Spencer's clearly making an effort to get to know me, and there's this huge part of my life that I'm scared to share with him.

Uncle Roy could care less if I tell the world I'm an exorcist—he doesn't think there's anything wrong with it.

But that's easy for him to say—he doesn't go to high school. It's just lucky for me that people who are in need of our services don't want the world to know they've been possessed. So far, I've been able to keep it under wraps.

Spencer pulls up to the curb in front of my house. The sound of the windshield wipers zipping back and forth fills the increasingly awkward silence between us.

"Well," I say, unbuckling my seatbelt. "Thanks for bringing me home."

"No problem." Spencer's eyes dart to the house, then back to me. House, back to me.

House.

Back to me.

My heart begins to race. Is he thinking about kissing me? I think he is.

"Shelby?" This time, it's Spencer's voice that squeaks. We stare at each other just long enough for it to become really painful, then he clears his throat. He flushes and leans forward to fiddle with the air vents again, and I know that he's lost his nerve.

I'm certainly no braver. I may be able to face down a demon, but the idea of making a move on Spencer is way scarier.

I grab my messenger bag and climb out of the car. I run through the rain to the front porch, and when I turn around,

Spencer is still sitting in his car at the curb. I'm too far away to see the expression on his face, but I can tell that he's looking at me.

Part of me wants to run back, gather my courage, and kiss him. But by the time I've convinced myself to do it, he's already pulling away. So I head inside, dropping my bag near the door.

The house has that empty feeling, the type of silence that you only get when you're completely alone. My throat tightens. I hate being home alone. It's much harder to distract myself from my mom, because she's all around me. She's here in the books that line our shelves, the blue rag rug she was so proud of finding at a thrift store, the horseshoes she hung over every doorway that she insisted would bring us good luck.

I go into the living room and plunk down in Uncle Roy's ugly old recliner, running my hands over the brown velour arms. My mom always said the chair was an eyesore, that it belonged in the dump, but more than once I found her curled up in it, reading a book. Just like that day we had our worst fight, the one that I don't like to think about but that continues to surface whenever I have a quiet moment.

I was hoping to sneak past her when I got home that evening. I was not in a good mood. I'd been seeing this guy,

Aaron, for a couple of months, and he'd just dumped me, right in the middle of dinner. All I wanted was to retreat to my room, where I could start the process of getting over him by throwing everything that even remotely reminded me of him into the trash.

"Shelby?" My mom said.

I took a deep breath, hoping she wouldn't notice that my eyes were swollen. But, of course, she noticed. My mom notices everything.

"Honey, what's wrong?" She set down her book and made a move to stand up, but I held out my hand to stop her.

"I'm fine."

Maybe everything would have turned out differently if I'd just been honest with her, if I'd let her comfort me instead of turning on her like a trapped animal.

Worry lines appeared on her forehead. "You're clearly not fine."

"Mom. Please."

I was struggling to hold back the tears and I just wanted to be alone, but she wouldn't let it go. She couldn't ever let it go, at least not when it came to me.

"Is it Aaron?"

It was the logical conclusion, but it infuriated me that she'd figured it out so quickly. And suddenly I couldn't hold back anymore. All the emotion that I was trying so hard to contain came rushing out of me, all directed at the one person who I just expected would always be there to take it.

"Oh my God, can you just stop?" I said, crossing my arms. "This is why Dad left, right? You drove him away with all your nagging."

This was the lowest blow, because I knew that this, in fact, was the reason my dad gave as he was packing up his convertible two years ago. It wasn't true—his leaving had more to do with the woman waiting for him in California than in my mom asking him, repeatedly, to take out the garbage—but I could tell from the hurt on her face that the words had found their mark.

My mom paled. "Shelby—"

"Seriously," I said, not letting her get a word in. The tears were coming now, and I swiped angrily at my face. I was spinning out of control, and I didn't know how to reign it in. "Maybe I should just go live with him."

It didn't matter that I regretted the words as soon as they were out of my mouth. They were out there, and I couldn't take them back.

"I'm staying at Vanessa's tonight," I said.

My mom nodded. "You know what? That's probably a good idea," she said. Her face tight, she picked up her book and started to read.

I ran down the hall. *Not my fault*, I thought, already feeling guilty. I threw some pajamas into my bag, along with my toothbrush. *She shouldn't have pushed me.*

Still, I expected her to try to stop me from leaving, but she didn't even look my way as I stormed out of the house. She just let me go.

And the next morning she was gone.

Chapter

7

UNCLE ROY is standing in front of the open fridge when I walk into the kitchen the next morning. He's wearing his blue velvet robe and slippers that have seen better days. "I could swear we had some strawberry jam left."

"I threw it out," I say, going over to stand beside him. "Too much sugar." I find a tub of low-fat cottage cheese buried in the back of the fridge and hand it to him.

He frowns. "Am I meant to put this on my toast?"

"Whatever strikes your fancy," I say, patting his arm.

"What strikes my fancy is strawberry jam." He removes two pieces of sunflower seed bread from the toaster with a resigned sigh, then carries his breakfast over to the table and sits down.

He pops open the tub of cottage cheese and glowers at the contents. He picks up his knife and spreads a thin layer on his toast. He looks so dejected that I can't help but feel a bit guilty. I take the cinnamon out of the cupboard and bring it over to him.

"Where are you off to in such a rush?" he says as I pick up my messenger bag.

"I have to leave a bit early." So I can grab a chocolate-chip muffin on the way to school.

I swear, Uncle Roy's a mind reader, because he sprinkles a light dusting of cinnamon on the toast, then holds it out to me. "Well, you can't start the day without breakfast," he says. "Most important meal of the day, as you know."

I do feel bad leaving him to eat on his own, so I take the toast and sit down across from him. The cinnamon doesn't quite cover up the odor of the cottage cheese, which, I have to admit, does not smell at all appealing. It's also superclumpy, and my stomach churns just looking at it.

But I take a bite, because maybe it doesn't taste as bad

as it smells/looks, and besides, I want to set a good example. If I can't eat this stuff, then I guess I can't expect him to.

"Mmm," I say, struggling to keep my face blank. I chew and swallow as fast as I can, because, honestly, whoever thought cottage cheese was a good idea?

Uncle Roy starts to laugh, and that sets me off. Pretty soon, we're both giggling.

"Okay, fine," I say, pushing my plate away. "It's gross. Happy?"

Uncle Roy wipes his eyes. "Yes," he says. "Now, how about I make us some scrambled eggs?"

The laughter dies in my throat as he goes to the fridge to get some eggs. Uncle Roy is a scrambled egg master chef. He used to make them for my mom and me every weekend, but we haven't had them once since she left.

I swallow, trying to work up the nerve to ask him if he's heard from her. I don't like to open this door often because I don't want to hear that she's called him and not me. But I can't help myself.

"Can I ask you something? About Mom?"

Uncle Roy stiffens slightly. "Of course," he says as he cracks the eggs into a silver bowl. I'm not sure if his hand is shaking because he's so old or because he's not comfortable with me asking questions. Maybe it's a little bit of both.

"When do you think she'll be back?"

He concentrates on whisking the eggs. "Shelby, I know these past few months have been hard on you," he says. All traces of his smile are gone. "I know you miss her. I miss Robin, too. Very much. But I'm afraid I can't tell you much more than that she'll be back soon."

It's no more than I expected him to say—it's what he's told me a hundred times since she left—but still, I'm disappointed. I know that he knows something happened with my mom that night, but he's never pressed me for details. And I'm so grateful, because at this point, it wouldn't take much to break me.

I watch Uncle Roy fold shredded Jack cheese into the egg mixture, then pour it into a cast-iron pan. It's all too much, having breakfast without my mom. I have to get out of here. The kitchen suddenly feels too small, and I can feel tears pushing at the back of my eyes.

"Um, I just remembered, I have a geometry test first thing," I say, standing up and grabbing my bag. I hear Uncle Roy calling my name as I rush down the hall, but I don't stop. If I stop, I'll tell him everything, and I can't bear to see the look of disappointment on his face when he finds out the truth.

✗ ✗

I've become an expert at pushing my emotions way down deep, where I don't have to deal with them, so by the time lunch rolls around and Vanessa and I are parked on the front steps outside of the school, I'm no longer thinking about this morning.

"I can't believe you haven't noticed that I dyed my hair," Vanessa says.

"What?" I glance at her, but so far as I can tell, her hair is the same shiny black it always is.

She pulls an electric-blue curl from underneath her thick nest of hair and twirls it in her fingers. "I'm thinking about dying my entire head this color."

"Cool."

She sighs. I haven't given her the reaction she's looking for, but I'm not sure what it is she wants me to say. Plus, I'm distracted by the sight of Grayson O'Neill, Spencer's friend, who's trying to get Vanessa's attention by doing some kind of skateboard trick off the curb in front of the school. He's supercute—tall with dark-red hair, built like a basketball player—but he's a junior, and Vanessa has some dumb rule about not dating anyone younger than she is, so she won't give him the time of day. Though, she should, because he's really nice. He smiles at us and I raise my hand to wave, but Vanessa, who is obviously only pretending not to notice what he's up to, smacks it down.

"Don't encourage him," she says, sliding closer to me as Ms. Caplan, our English teacher, makes her way up the stairs.

Ms. C isn't the most "with it" teacher, but there's something extra off about her today. She's more disheveled than usual; her blouse is buttoned up incorrectly, and her red hair doesn't look like it's seen a brush in days. She's mumbling to herself, and she's walking funny, this strange kind of Frankenstein walk. She also reeks like rotten eggs.

"Oh my God, what is that heinous smell?" Vanessa gags and claps her hand over her nose. She glances at me, wide-eyed. "Did Ms. C just cut one? Seriously, what kind of world are we living in?"

Maybe Ms. C smells bad for other reasons, I tell myself. Not every terrible smell is the work of the devil. It doesn't necessarily mean she's possessed.

I am worrying needlessly.

Everything is fine.

But I have a twisty feeling in my stomach, the one I only get when I'm in the presence of an evil spirit.

Okay, so what would Uncle Roy want me to do?

Well, he would definitely not want me to perform an exorcism on my own. I know this, and yet, here I am at my locker two minutes later, rummaging in my backpack for my silver crucifix. There's no time to call him; the end-of-lunch bell is going to ring in five minutes. I don't need his help, anyway, because despite what he thinks, I can do this myself.

I peer through the small window in the door to

Ms. Caplan's classroom. She's sitting at her desk, staring into space. I watch her for a few minutes, but she doesn't move. She just sits there. Staring.

Maybe she's not possessed. Maybe she's just having a really bad day.

I've almost convinced myself that I've overreacted when Ms. C's head suddenly twists toward me. Her face is blank, freakily devoid of all expression, and her eyes have turned completely black.

Well, that settles it, then.

I lean against the door and take a deep breath. My plan— and I think it's a pretty good one—is to spray her with holy water from a safe distance and hope that distracts her long enough so that I can rush in and handcuff her to the arm-rest on her rolling chair. Once she's secured, I'll start the incantation.

And voilà! Exorcism complete. Just in time for class to start.

I dig my bejeweled purple spray bottle of holy water out of my bag and hide it behind my back. Then I take another deep breath and push open the door. My heart thunders in my chest as whatever has an evil hold on Ms. C watches me with its dead shark eyes.

I think about locking the door so no one can barge in,

but I don't want to turn my back on her. I need to get a bit closer in order to effectively spray her, but not so close that she can grab me if she figures out what I'm up to.

"Hi, Ms. Caplan," I say. "I have some questions about the homework assignment." My hands are shaking. I tighten my grip on the spray bottle as I slowly walk toward her.

Almost there.

One more step.

When I'm in front of her desk, I whip out the spray bottle and start squirting. Holy water is very powerful—if you are possessed, it will do a number on your skin. Sure enough, steam starts to rise from a spot near her elbow. Ms. C lets out an inhuman scream and shoots out of her chair, at least three feet into the air.

And it's at that moment that I realize my handcuffs are buried in the bottom of my bag and I have zero point zero seconds to dig them out. Restraining her is not going to be an option.

I can hear Uncle Roy's voice in my head, chastising me for making such a rookie mistake.

Ms. C lands on top of her desk, crouched on all fours like an animal. She snarls, and I try not to gag. A public bathroom that hasn't been cleaned in a few weeks probably smells better than her breath.

I spray her again, this time right between the eyes. She screams even louder and covers her face with her hands. Steam pours out from between her fingers.

Okay, so the screaming has got to stop; it's definitely going to draw attention. It's probably only a matter of seconds before someone comes into the room to find out who's being murdered. I need to start the exorcism ASAP.

I drop the spray bottle and hold up my crucifix. *"Deus, in nómine tuo salvum me fac, et virtúte tua age causam meam,"* I say, putting as much force into the words as possible. *"Deus, audi oratiónem meam; áuribus pércipe verba oris mei."*

Ms. C leaps off the desk. She soars over my head and lands directly behind me with a soft thud. She's standing so close, I can feel her hot breath on my neck. I shudder. I have never been so afraid in my life. The lesson that Uncle Roy has drummed into me more than any other is to never turn your back on a demon.

Swallowing, I make myself turn around.

Ms. C is standing mere inches from me, her face twisted with a smile so terrible, I'm sure it will give me nightmares for the rest of my life. Which, given how this exorcism is going, might only be a few more minutes.

"Nam supérbi insurréxerunt contra me—" My voice wobbles. The demon picks up on my wavering confidence and pushes me, sending me crashing to the floor. My knee knocks hard

against the metal leg of her desk. She takes a run for the window. Then she leaps through it in a pretty impressive feat of acrobatics. I'm super-relieved that she didn't kill me but also terrified, because we are on the third floor and I really don't want to have to explain why my English teacher just threw herself out the window. Also, Ms. C is a very nice person and I really hope that she isn't dead.

The bell rings. I stand up, wincing at the pain in my left knee, and hobble over to the window. The classroom is at the side of the school, overlooking the Dumpsters. Maybe she landed in one of them—on the bright side, she won't smell any worse than she already does. But when I look out the window, there's no sign of Ms. C.

She's gone.

I'm in so much trouble.

Chapter

8

OKAY, *so that didn't go as planned*, I think as the bell rings. But I can still make it right. I just need to find Ms. C.

Think. Think! If I were a demon, where would I go?

I pull out my phone as I'm walking out of the school and do a quick search for her address. There's a V. Caplan who lives only a few blocks away. I'll start there. Maybe she went home to wash the holy water out of her eyes.

Just as I'm crossing the parking lot, I see Mr. Hanover,

the principal, walking toward me. Unfortunately, he sees me, too.

"The bell rang three minutes ago, Ms. Black," he says. "Where are you supposed to be?"

I swallow. "Oh, um," I say. I madly cast around in my brain for a believable excuse, but I'm not great at thinking on my feet, especially when I'm face-to-face with a frowning principal. My shoulders sag. "Bio."

"Well, as I'm sure you know, our biology classes are actually held *inside* the school," he says. "Which means you need to be going into the school instead of away from it. I'm heading there myself. I'll walk you in."

I'm really beginning to panic—I have to get to Ms. C—but I'm left with no option other than to obediently follow Mr. Hanover into the school. If he only knew what was at stake—that I was actually leaving the school grounds so I can save the soul of one of his best teachers and not just because I want to skip bio. But I'm pretty sure he won't believe me if I tell him that.

Mr. Hanover keeps his eyes on me until I disappear around the corner past the main office. But instead of going to class, I duck behind a potted ficus. If I hang out here for a few minutes, hopefully he'll leave and I can finally get on my way.

"Have you seen Violet, by any chance?" I hear him ask

Melody, the school receptionist. "She didn't show up to class."

Violet Caplan.

V. Caplan.

V for victory! The address I found has to be hers. Now I'm even more determined to get to her house.

Melody murmurs something that I can't quite catch.

Mr. Hanover sighs. "All right, well, if you see her, send her up. I'll take over until she gets here." He sounds as excited about the prospect of teaching her English class as he would about getting a rectal exam.

Once his footsteps retreat down the hall, I peer around the corner to make sure Melody isn't paying attention, then I dart out the door. I hobble-run the whole way to Ms. C's house. Clearly I need to work on my cardio, because by the time I get there, I am out of breath and sweaty and I'm sure I smell as bad as any demon.

But I can't worry about that now.

The first flutters of panic begin to set in. Her driveway is empty, but maybe she left her car at the school or parked out back or something.

The front door is painted a cheery yellow. I take my crucifix out of my bag just in case she is inside, then I glance over my shoulder to make sure no one is around. I bend down and check underneath the black mat with *Friends Welcome* written on it in white cursive script. Sure enough, there's a key.

I pick it up, making a mental note to tell Ms. C once I've returned her to herself that she shouldn't leave her spare key in such an obvious place, where anyone can find it. I slide the key into the lock and push the door open. As it slowly creaks on its hinges, revealing the inside of her house, my heart stutters to a stop.

Her living room is completely trashed. I think there would be less damage if a tornado had gone through. Stuffing spills out of the back of the floral couch, like someone ripped into it with a knife. Or claws. The legs of the coffee table are broken right off and the glass top is shattered. The worst part, though, the part that makes the hair on the back of my neck stand on end, is the graffiti.

I start to shake. It's hard to imagine my sweet English teacher spraying Satanic symbols on her walls. But if whatever has a hold on her is capable of this, then it's strong enough to wreak great damage. If I don't find her soon, then whatever she does, whoever she hurts, is going to be my fault.

Evil has a vibration—we were built to sense it, but most people lose the ability somewhere along the way. I can feel it now, vibrating through every part of my body. I know I shouldn't go any farther inside the house, but I'm hoping she left a clue. It's like I'm in a horror movie. I'm the oblivious girl who makes the decision to press on, the girl who is too dumb to know when to turn around.

The girl who always ends up dead.

I head down the hall toward the kitchen, holding my crucifix out in front of me like a weapon. I suddenly step on something that crunches underneath my St. Joseph's regulation loafer. I glance down and see Ms. C's horn-rimmed glasses, snapped cleanly in two.

So the good news is that she's definitely been home. She was wearing these glasses when I saw her in her classroom. The bad news is that I've broken them beyond repair.

Hopefully she won't hold this against me. I really need a good grade in English this semester.

The kitchen, as it turns out, is even worse than the living room; there are stacks of unwashed dishes in the sink, covered with a film of mold. The refrigerator door is wide open and all the food inside is spoiled. I pick up a carton of milk and give it a shake, and I can feel it clumping inside, which, I'm not going to lie, makes me gag. The kitchen table has an axe sticking out of the middle of it, which is just plain freaky, and I'm pretty sure that the tiny brown pellets spread all over her counters are not raisins but the work of mice.

My heart sinks. How long has Ms. C been living like this? This did not happen overnight. Has she been possessed for a while and I just missed the signs?

I should definitely pay more attention to my teachers.

I notice a blue flyer on the kitchen table. It's advertising for some bar called El Diablo.

El Diablo.

The Devil.

I wonder if this is where Ms. C was heading. I fold the flyer and tuck it in the back pocket of my jeans. It's the only lead I have, and I guess I should check it out.

Unfortunately, this poses a major problem for me. Even if I had a fake ID, I doubt any bouncer would buy that I'm twenty-one. Honestly, I think I'm out of my depth.

There's no way around it.

I have to call Uncle Roy.

Chapter

9

ASIDE FROM the occasional grunt, Uncle Roy is mostly silent while I explain the situation, not commenting even as I try to convince him that my actions potentially prevented a classroom full of schoolchildren from crossing paths with an actual demon.

I'm not looking for a medal or anything, but some appreciation of the fact that I saved a bunch of innocent people would be nice.

"I mean, it was definitely a learning experience," I say, trying to inject lightness into my tone. "And the best way to learn is by doing, right?"

Silence.

More silence.

Still more silence.

I finally break. "Okay, so I probably shouldn't have tried to exorcise her on my own," I admit. "But I've been training for five months. I thought I had it handled." I would have had it handled if Ms. C hadn't jumped out the window. Of course, she wouldn't have jumped out the window if I'd managed to restrain her, but I don't want to bring that to Uncle Roy's attention. Besides, I'm sure he's already made note of it.

"This isn't a game, Shelby." Uncle Roy's voice is a blade of anger slicing right through me. He's been mad at me before—plenty of times—but I've never heard him quite this worked up.

My face starts to burn. "I know it's not a game. I was only trying to help." I know I screwed up, but he never gives me any credit. I don't know why he's so bent on me becoming an exorcist when he clearly doesn't trust me to do the job.

"We'll discuss this later," he says. "Right now, we need to find this poor woman."

✗ ✗

Ten minutes later, Uncle Roy pulls up in front of Ms. C's house. I climb into the passenger seat and steal a look at him. His lips are pressed together so tightly that they're almost nonexistent, and his thick white eyebrows have settled so low over his eyes that I wonder how he can even see.

I hand him the flyer I found in Ms. C's kitchen. "I think she might have gone here."

He glances at it, and his already turned-down mouth turns down even farther. "I know the place."

I'm surprised by this. Not judging, but a dive bar doesn't seem like the type of place a priest would know about. Then again, Uncle Roy isn't an average priest.

He tells me that he's going to drop me off at school, but when I point out that he doesn't know what Ms. Caplan looks like and therefore will never be able to find her without my help, he grudgingly agrees to let me tag along. Trust me, I'm not superexcited to be spending time with him right now, but I started this, so I feel like I have to be there to finish it. Or at least watch him finish it, because there is zero chance he'll let me try to exorcise her again.

Uncle Roy doesn't like to listen to music in the car, so I'm stuck inside my own head for the entire drive, and it's not exactly the best place to be right now. My stomach clenches as I think about how thoroughly the demon destroyed Ms. C's house and how it's now working on destroying her soul.

The longer a demon is inside its host, the stronger it becomes—the one that has a hold on Ms. C is clearly strong, so I'll bet it's been inside her for a while, just waiting to come out. And the more time a demon spends in there, the more damage it can do. Sometimes, the damage is permanent. We exorcised this guy, Peter Satterley, a few months ago. He'd been possessed for a while, and by the time we got to him, his soul had already been pretty much obliterated by his demon-in-residence. Peter was only in his forties, and he ended up in a long-term care facility because he wasn't able to care for himself. It's awful and sad, and I can't bear the idea of that happening to anyone else.

Please, God, don't let the same thing happen to Ms. C.

Uncle Roy parks the car. A row of motorcycles are parked in a neat line in front of an old, crumbly building with steel bars on the windows. A red neon sign depicting the devil hangs over the scarred metal door.

"Fun place," I say. My heart starts to bump against my ribs.

Uncle Roy must sense my fear, because he grasps my hand. "Stay close to me," he says. "And, Shelby, if this goes sideways, I need you to promise me that you'll run."

"What? No way. I'm not going to leave you behind—"

"Promise me, Shelby," he says, and I wince as he tightens his grip on my fingers. Uncle Roy may be old, but he's hella strong.

If something bad happens to him, what will happen to me? As curmudgeonly as he can be, I don't want to lose him.

"All right, fine," I say. "I promise."

He releases my hand, and I shake out my fingers. He closes his eyes and says a quick prayer of protection, then, with a weary sigh, he says, "Let's get this over with."

We climb out of the car. I grab my crucifix and spray bottle of holy water out of my bag as Uncle Roy opens the door to the gates of hell. Or El Diablo, as it's more commonly known.

Perhaps unsurprisingly, the place reeks of cigarette smoke and hard liquor. Oh, and the putrid stink of demon.

We're in the right place.

It's so dark, it takes a minute for my eyes to adjust. When they do, I can see that the bar is mostly empty aside from a few tough-looking men sitting at tables scattered around the room. Every one of them turns to stare at us, the priest and the underage girl in a Catholic school uniform.

I move closer to Uncle Roy. Perhaps we should have considered coming undercover.

"What do you want?" a growly voice says. A giant man

with scraggly brown hair and a long brown beard that dusts the top of his rounded stomach lumbers toward us.

"We're looking for someone," Uncle Roy says calmly. "A woman."

"She's about this tall." I hold my hand up to my shoulder. "And she has curly red hair."

And she's possessed. But he doesn't need to know that.

The man glares at me, his eyes narrowed. I smile, hoping that, if I'm friendly, I can crack his scary exterior, but he doesn't smile back.

"Um . . . she's wearing a blue shirt." Seriously, there aren't that many people in here—you'd think he'd pick up on my description.

"I don't want any trouble," the man says.

"We're not here to make trouble," Uncle Roy replies. "We're here to prevent it." The man strokes his beard, studying us. He seems to be making his mind up about something. Finally, he grunts and says, "Come with me."

He leads us across the club, winding his way past a table filled with men in leather vests with red bandanas tied around their heads. They're clearly a gang, the owners of the motorcycles parked out front. I accidentally make eye contact with one of them; he grins at me in a way that makes my skin crawl.

Those evil vibrations I mentioned earlier? El Diablo is full of them.

The man stops outside of the ladies' room. "She's been in there an awful long time," he says. "If she's plugged my toilet, I'm not going to be a happy camper." He's about to knock, but Uncle Roy grabs his hand before he can make contact with the door.

"Wait." Uncle Roy removes the handcuffs from his pocket and gives them to me. "Shelby, as soon as we go in, check for anything we can cuff her to. Make sure it's something secure, preferably something made of iron. The tap in the sink, maybe," he says.

Iron is a magical substance that repels demons, for reasons I've long forgotten.

"What kind of sick game are you playing at?" the man asks, his eyes widening at the handcuffs. "Are you even a real priest?"

"I assure you, sir, I am indeed a priest," Uncle Roy says. "And I'm just doing my job. Now, if you'll kindly step aside. . . ."

The man clearly doesn't know what to make of the situation, but Uncle Roy is so bossy that he moves out of the way. Uncle Roy grasps the large silver crucifix hanging around his neck, holding it out in front of him as he pushes open the door.

The smell of sulfur hits us like a wave. It's so strong that it makes my eyes water. The man gags and claps his hand over his nose.

The bathroom is small, no bigger than a cell. The mirror above the rust-stained sink is cracked, like someone punched it, and the toilet is missing its seat.

There are no windows—and no Ms. C.

"Huh. She must have snuck out," the man says from behind his hand.

But Uncle Roy has gone completely still. He slowly gazes up at the ceiling, and every hair on my body stands up. Suddenly I know, even without looking, that Ms. C is still in the room.

And, sure enough, when I find the courage to look upward, there she is, hanging upside down, directly above us, like something right out of a vampire movie.

"What the hell?" The man's eyes bulge. "What is she on?"

"She's not on anything. This woman is possessed," Uncle Roy says, gesturing for my spray bottle.

"I told you, I don't want no trouble!" The man makes a grab for the bottle. Obviously he's not thinking clearly, because if he was, he'd know that *not* spraying her is going to cause way more trouble.

"Sir, you need to let us help her," Uncle Roy says, holding the bottle out of his reach.

"Or what?" he snarls.

At that moment, Ms. C reaches down and lifts the man off the ground by his long dark hair. He screams, swatting at her with his meaty fists, but she holds him up as if he weighs no more than a sparrow.

"Or that," Uncle Roy says.

Ms. C lets him go, and the man falls in a heap, a handful of his hair still in her hand. He crab-walks out of the bathroom, his eyes lit with terror.

Who's the big, bad, scary guy now?

I laugh because, honestly? It's funny. At least until Uncle Roy roughly nudges me out of the way.

"Stand back, please," Uncle Roy says. He aims the spray bottle at Ms. C's leg and fires. She screams as curls of steam rise off her shin and then drops to the ground, crouching like she's about to pounce. Then she snarls, and her lips peel back to show her teeth. Her eyes are glowing and super-red. Her face is red, too, right in the spot where I squirted her with holy water earlier.

Yikes. I hope that isn't permanent.

"*Deus, audi oratiónem meam; áuribus pércipe verba oris mei,*" Uncle Roy bellows, his voice echoing off the grungy tile walls.

As soon as he starts the incantation, Ms. C's body contorts in a way that reminds me of those crazy talented acrobats in Cirque du Soleil. She practically does a cartwheel off the wall, and I can't help but be impressed by how limber she is. I mean, she has to be at least thirty years old, but from the way she's moving, she could probably medal in the Olympics.

"*Nam supérbi insurréxerunt contra me . . .*" Uncle Roy glances at me, an exasperated expression on his face.

What?

Oh, right. The handcuffs.

". . . *et violénti quæsierunt vitam meam. . . .*" As he slowly moves closer to Ms. C, I scan the bathroom for something made of iron. The taps are chipped white porcelain, so that's not great news. But I guess they're going to have to do.

Ms. C scrambles to try to get away from us, but there's really nowhere for her to go—she's trapped between the sink and the toilet. I guess that bit of superhuman gymnastics took a lot out of her, because she's starting to slow down, which is a good sign. It means that the demon is getting tired.

At this point I don't think she has the strength to levitate, so the handcuffs are probably overkill, but Uncle Roy must want to make this a "teachable moment" because he gestures for me to move in on her.

"Grab her wrist," he barks.

While Uncle Roy distracts her with the incantation, I clamp the handcuff over one of Ms. C's bone-thin wrists. Her skin is burning up, but whether that's from the hellfire burning inside of her or from her aerobic display, it's impossible to know. Before I can attach the other end of the handcuffs to the tap, Ms. C starts to convulse. Her whole body gives one final, violent twist, then relaxes, like a marionette that's just had its strings cut. The suddenness of the movement causes her to face-plant right into the toilet.

Her head.

Is in.

The toilet.

Oh my God.

I make a move to help her, but Uncle Roy holds up a finger, his way of telling me to wait. He watches Ms. C for a minute before walking over and poking her in the shoulder with his crucifix. Ms. C groans, but she doesn't spontaneously combust, so it seems that the demon has officially been expelled.

Yay us!

Or yay Uncle Roy, anyway.

Ms. Caplan struggles to sit up. The ends of her hair are wet with toilet water.

"It's okay, Ms. Caplan. It's me, Shelby."

"Shelby? What on earth . . . ?" She squints at me. "Where are my glasses? I can't see anything without my glasses."

"Um, I'm not sure," I say, thinking of how easily her glasses snapped underneath my loafer earlier.

"And what's that awful smell?" Ms. C wrinkles her nose.

I don't want to tell her that it's her. I don't want to freak her out any more than is necessary.

"It's a long story," I say, helping her to her feet.

I introduce her to Uncle Roy. He puts his arm around her, and we lead her, confused and unsteady, out of the bar and into the light.

Chapter

10

DROPPING MS. C off at home isn't an option given the demon-wrecked state of her place, so Uncle Roy has convinced her that we should take her to her sister's house. I'm sitting beside her in the back seat.

Uncle Roy's just patiently explained the day's events to her for the third time, but Ms. C seems to think he's making it all up. Every time he says the word *demon*, she just shakes her head.

"I know it's a lot to take in, Violet," he says.

"But I don't even believe in demons," she replies, kneading her hands together. "I don't believe in anything! I'm an atheist!"

Well, atheism doesn't explain the graffiti all over her living room walls or how she was able to hang from the ceiling of that bathroom like a spider. It also doesn't explain why she's teaching at a Catholic school, but that's a question for another day.

Ms. C's face brightens. "Maybe I had a seizure."

"Maybe we should just take her home," I say to Uncle Roy.

He glares at me in the rearview mirror. "Shelby."

"What?" She'd hardly be able to deny that something evil was up when she saw the ax sticking out of her kitchen table.

Ms. C turns to face me. She obviously can't see anything without her glasses, because although she's looking in my direction, her eyes are unfocused and it's pretty clear that she's not really seeing me. Now that the demon is gone, the burns on her face have disappeared, so she's back to normal. Ish.

"Tell me again why I can't go home," she says, sounding suspicious.

I've already told her why six times, but Uncle Roy claims

that short-term memory loss is completely normal after a possession, so I'm trying my best to be patient with her.

"Your house needs to be fumigated," I say. This is not really a lie; Uncle Roy does need to give the house a serious spiritual cleansing before she can live there again.

Ms. C doesn't ask how on earth I know that her house needs to be fumigated. Hopefully by the time she returns to her senses, she won't remember this conversation. Or my role in any of this, for that matter.

Uncle Roy turns onto a wide, tree-lined street. Ms. Caplan points out her sister's house, a huge white Victorian with a lawn the size of a postage stamp. Uncle Roy instructs me to stay put. He helps Ms. C climb out of the car. Her legs are still pretty shaky, so he slides his arm around her and walks her up to the front door.

Ms. Caplan's sister opens the door. I can't imagine what Uncle Roy is telling her to explain why they're on her doorstep, but whatever it is, from the concerned look on her face, it's clear that she buys it. She wraps an arm around Ms. C's shoulders and leads her inside.

I'm so tired. This day has kicked my butt. I let my eyes drift shut for a moment, and I must fall asleep, because the next time I open my eyes, we're in front of Ms. C's house.

"You're going to do the cleansing now?" I ask, yawning. Uncle Roy's been exhausted after exorcisms lately, so I figured he'd want a break before he tackled chasing the evil spirits out of Ms. C's place.

"Yes," he says. "I'll be doing that while you put her house back in order."

I sit up, suddenly wide-awake. "In order? As in clean up?"

He smiles tightly. "Who did you think was going to do it?"

I guess I never thought about it.

Silly me.

✖ ✖

Three hours later, Ms. C's house is almost back to normal. Or what we assume is normal—maybe Ms. C is a slob who never does her dishes. In that case, we've just given her free housekeeping services.

I haul the last of the four trash bags filled with downy white stuffing from the decorative pillows in her bedroom down the stairs. Uncle Roy is in the living room, talking to a man in paint-splattered jeans.

The man stares uneasily at the graffiti on the wall. "You're going to need at least two coats of primer to cover that."

"Fine," Uncle Roy says. "Can you match the yellow?"

The painter nods. "I think I can get pretty close."

We are trying to put Ms. C's place back together as closely as possible, but there are some things that just can't be fixed, like her coffee table. I swept up the glass, and we carried the broken metal legs out to Uncle Roy's car—which is now filled with garbage, because apparently we can't leave twenty Hefty bags on the curb.

The painter heads out to his van to get his supplies. I don't know how Uncle Roy found him so quickly. I feel guilty that he's paying for it out of his own pocket, but honestly, I don't think I could have faced painting all night.

I drop the trash bag of pillow fluff near the door and plunk down onto the couch. Uncle Roy has fixed duct tape over the claw marks. If the couch fit in his car, I'd suggest we take it to the dump.

"Are we done? I'm exhausted."

"You know who's not exhausted?" Uncle Roy says, leaning down to remove his flask of holy water from his doctor's bag. "The devil."

I groan and let my head flop against the back of the couch. "Can't we have one conversation that doesn't revolve around demons?"

"When we get rid of them, we can talk about anything you like," he says, uncapping the flask. He walks around the room, sprinkling holy water in every corner.

I cross my arms. While I'm glad that we helped Ms. C, there will always be someone who needs us, and the responsibility of that makes me feel weighted down. No matter what

Uncle Roy says, we will never get rid of all the demons, ever, because they are everywhere and always have been. And they always will be.

And suddenly it all just feels like too much.

"Maybe we need to take a few days off," I say.

Uncle Roy frowns, his eyebrows gathering together in the middle of his forehead like a long white caterpillar. "Shelby, you know that even a single day can make a difference."

My face heats up. I know he's referring to Peter Satterley and what happened to him.

"If anything, we're in even greater demand now." He turns around and shakes holy water near the entrance to the room. "There's a particularly nasty demon that's been causing a lot of havoc lately." His back is to me, so I can't read his expression, but his voice sounds strange. "I believe the possessed individual is a portal to the underworld."

My stomach drops. I didn't even know that was possible. "Like a doorway for other demons to come through?"

He nods. "There are several known portals across the Pacific Northwest," he says. "Physical locations that have been cordoned off to keep the public from accidentally stumbling across them. However, this is the first case I've come across where the portal is an actual person."

"What does that mean?"

He turns around to face me. His expression is grave. "It means that unless we can find a way to stop it, the city will soon be overrun by demons."

I stare at him, wide-eyed. "And you never mentioned this before because . . . ?"

"I wasn't entirely sure until recently." He bends down to slip his flask of holy water back into his doctor's bag. "And I didn't want to worry you."

He didn't want to worry me? It's a little late for that.

"So how does this portal work, exactly?" I ask.

Uncle Roy grimaces. "Through touch," he says. "If this person grabs on to someone for more than a minute or two, then a conduit is created. The demonic spirit can travel through that person and into the other body."

I fold my hands together to keep them from shaking, trying to fight down the tide of panic rising inside of me. "There are, like, hundreds of priests in Seattle. Some of them must be willing to help us."

"Not all of them do exorcisms," he says. "And, quite frankly, the other priests I've approached don't believe that it's possible for a portal to be a person. I'm fairly certain that they think I'm losing my mind."

I sit up, indignant. Uncle Roy may be old, but his mind is still sharp. If he believes this person is a portal, then they're a portal.

"Then we'll just have to take care of it ourselves," I say.

He shakes his head. "Shelby, I told you this so you would understand the seriousness of the situation," he says. "But this is something you can't help me with."

I open my mouth to argue—exactly how does he expect to tackle a demon portal on his own?—but he cuts me off.

"It's not up for discussion," he says.

I scowl at him. Okay, I know Ms. C's exorcism didn't go according to plan, but what's the point of training me if he doesn't think I can help him?

He glances around the room. "I think our work here is done," he says, picking up his doctor's bag.

I stand up. The place looks a lot better than when we arrived, but there's no way Ms. C will be able to ignore the missing coffee table or the duct tape holding her couch together. And there's no way I can ignore the growing feeling that, no matter what Uncle Roy says, we are in way over our heads.

✗ ✗

Uncle Roy may have meant the work in Ms. C's house was done, but I still have to write the report on her exorcism. It's after eleven, and I'm so tired that my eyelids keep drooping shut, but I'm in the rectory, trying to commit everything that happened today to paper.

*. . . I started the incantation, and I almost had her, but then Ms. C jumped out of the window!!! There is no way I could have predicted she'd do that. **NO ONE** could have predicted she'd do that, even if that person has done a thousand exorcisms and thinks they know everything there is to know about demons.*

I sneak a glance at Uncle Roy. He's leaning back in his chair, eyes closed, his face as pale as the moon. Maybe it's just because he's relaxed, but it kind of looks like someone let all the air out of him.

Looking at him gives me a swoopy feeling in my stomach. I know Uncle Roy's a thousand years old, but if something were to happen to him, if he got sick . . .

There's nothing wrong with him. He's fine.

Still, I make a mental note to get all of the superfoods into his diet. Maybe there's a way I can disguise quinoa in brownies or something.

Moo must know I'm worried, because she snuggles deeper into my lap. Her soft, solid body and the motor-like sound of her purr reassure me. I push aside the bad thoughts and refocus my attention on the paper in front of me.

It's another half hour before I scribble my signature across the bottom of the page. It's not my best work, for sure, and I know I've given Uncle Roy plenty to pick at, but my fingers are cramping and I can't think of anything else to add.

I scratch Moo behind one ear and set her gently on the floor. I walk over and drop the report on the desk in front of Uncle Roy. Without even opening his eyes, he takes off the key he wears around his neck, the one that unlocks the filing cabinet, and hands it to me. I'm surprised because he always reads the reports before he files them, and he always puts them away himself, but I guess he's too tired tonight. Either that, or he thinks I can handle the responsibility and is starting to loosen the reigns.

Tired seems more likely, though.

I go over to the large, metal filing cabinet in the corner of the room and unlock the drawer marked *A–C*. I flip through the alphabetized files and shove *Caplan, V.* in the proper place. I'm about to shut the drawer when I notice the corner of one file sticking up slightly. I should just tuck it back in, respect the fact that these files are confidential, but what can I say? I'm nosy. So I pull it up and read the name. My breath catches.

Black, R.

It's probably just someone with the same first initial as

my mom. Black is a fairly common last name, after all. But then I flip open the file and see my mom's name scrawled in Uncle Roy's handwriting on the inside cover, and I begin to shake.

In an instant, I know that she's not in Italy.

Everything Uncle Roy has told me is a lie.

I glance over at him, fury coursing through me. His eyes are still closed, and now his mouth is hanging open, his jaw slack. I hear the soft whistle of his snores as I pull the report out as silently as I can.

Our reports are usually a page long. Two, max. My mom's is a stack of pages, roughly stapled together. I slip them underneath my shirt and into the waistband of my plaid skirt, then quietly close the filing cabinet. I walk back over to Uncle Roy and set the key on the desk. He startles awake, and our eyes meet. I look away before he can see my anger.

I have never gotten anything past him, ever, and for one second, I'm sure he's caught me. He knows I've taken my mom's file, and he's going to demand that I put it back before I've even had the chance to read it.

But he just yawns and rubs his eyes. "I guess it's time to turn in," he says, slipping the key on its silver chain back around his neck. He stands up, groaning as the joints in his knees pop, and I follow him out of the rectory.

On the walk back to the house, which is less than thirty feet, Uncle Roy notices me shivering. "Shelby, where is your jacket?"

It's not the night air that's causing me to shake. I've been blaming myself for my mom's disappearance for months. He let me believe that I'm the reason she left. "I'm fine." My voice sounds higher than normal, but he doesn't seem to notice.

The file starts to slip as we walk. I put a hand to my stomach to keep it from sliding down my leg and onto the ground.

"Are you hungry?" Uncle Roy asks. "I just realized that we forgot to eat dinner."

I didn't forget—I scarfed down a couple of granola bars I had stashed in my backpack when I was cleaning Ms. C's living room. "I'm fine," I say, kicking off my loafers just inside the front door. "It's been a long day. I just want to go to bed."

Uncle Roy pauses outside my room, like he's waiting for something. Probably for me to apologize for attempting to exorcise Ms. C on my own. Well, he can wait forever.

"Well, good night, then," he says.

I'm itching to dive into my mom's file, but I have to wait for Uncle Roy to get a glass of water from the kitchen. I wait for his bedroom door to close. And then I wait some more, because I'm afraid of what I'm about to read.

I pull the report out from my waistband and sit down on my bed. I run my hand over it. The paper is worn soft as old leather, like it's been read again and again and again. Uncle Roy's neat block letters fill up every inch of the pages.

I take a deep breath.

> **Case Number:** EX100-17-0092
> **Incident:** The Exorcism of Robin Black
> **Exorcist:** Father Roy Watson
>
> Second of December, approximately 2000 hours. My partner, Robin Black, asked me to attend a routine exorcism of one of our young parishioners, to be held in the boy's parents' home. Robin had attempted to expel the demon on her own several times previously with no success. She believed that in this particular case, the strength of two exorcists performing the incantation would be the most effective way to eject this stubborn demon and save the young man's soul.

I accompanied Robin to the house on the evening of December 2nd. We commenced the exorcism in much the same way we always do, however, as this was Robin's case, she took the lead. She is an experienced exorcist who is particularly good with children, and she typically handles all cases involving any clients under eighteen.

Everything was going well—it seemed Robin's hypothesis was correct, that two exorcists are better than one, at least when it came to the stranglehold this demon had on the boy.

We were almost through the exorcism and the demon was in the throes of finally being expelled when the young man began calling for his mother and Robin became distracted. She stumbled on the incantation. While it was only for a moment, it was enough for the demon to wrest back control. However, when the young man went limp a minute *later, I believed the exorcism to be successful. I encouraged Robin to finish the job and approach him with the holy water, but when I turned to face her, I could see that the demon had simply traded one body for another. Robin's eyes were black and soulless. She hissed at me, and before I could stop her, she ran out of the house and into the night.*

I feel like I'm going to be sick. Even though I knew from the second I found the file that my mom is possessed, it still hits me like a punch in the gut.

I guess Uncle Roy was hoping that he'd be able to fix her before I really felt her absence. But I've felt it every second that she's been gone. She left a huge hole in my life, one that no one else could ever fill. He knows that. He knows it, but he still didn't tell me the truth.

I take a deep breath, trying to calm down so I can finish reading the report. I need to know everything.

12-20-16. I tracked Robin to Pike Place Market, however I wasn't able to get

*close enough to her to effectively
exorcise her.*

*02-13-17. Capitol Hill. She recognized
me and ran away before I could get
near her. I have noticed a dramatic
increase in demonic activity in the city
these past two months, and I fear this
demon is responsible.*

*04-04-17. Belltown. Almost got close
enough to restrain her, but once again
she slipped out of my grasp before I
could put handcuffs on her. This demon
is proving more clever than most.*

Each page tells a similar story: Uncle Roy finds my mom, but she manages to elude him. He's seen her dozens of times over the past five months. I turn to the last page, which has an entry dated three weeks ago, and it almost stops my heart:

*If my suspicions are correct, then this
demon is a portal to the underworld. It*

is directly responsible for the rash of
possessions we've seen lately. This
demon must be stopped at any cost.

Oh my God.

My mom is the portal.

Chapter

11

I WAS awake most of the night, my mind flipping through every terrible situation that my mom could be in and all the havoc she's creating. I sweated so much, I soaked through my sheets. She's out there somewhere, alone and helpless, and Uncle Roy, the only person who can help her, has not been able to get close enough to exorcise her.

I'm not ready to confront Uncle Roy yet. I want to get out of the house before he wakes up, so even though it's just past sunrise, I get up and throw on jeans and a hoodie. My entire body is stiff with tension, and there's a throbbing in my temples from lack of sleep. I stuff my mom's file into my messenger bag and quietly open my bedroom door.

I can smell coffee brewing. Uncle Roy is banging around in the kitchen, making his breakfast. Seems like I'm not the only one who's having trouble sleeping. I guess that's what a guilty conscience gets you.

I go out the back door so I don't have to pass by him. Unfortunately, the only shoes that are back here are my mom's hideous, blue rubber gardening clogs. I hate these shoes—I always made fun of her for wearing them—but I can't help but smile, thinking how she would laugh if she knew I was being forced to put them on my feet.

I walk down to the doughnut shop a few blocks from our house. I have no appetite, but I have to get something if I'm going to kill time here, so I order a couple of apple fritters. I sit in a red vinyl booth and pore over my mom's file, looking for some kind of clue that Uncle Roy might have missed. Something that might lead me to her.

Two hours later, I'm no closer to an answer. My throat is raw from holding back tears. I am exhausted and over-whelmed, and I've never felt so helpless in my life. I imagine that this is how Uncle Roy's been feeling for the past five months, but instead of sympathy, anger floods through me. Because he didn't have to face this alone. I could have helped him. He should have told me. We could have been working together to find her.

I check my phone. I have three missed calls from Uncle Roy. He is usually up way before me, so I guess the fact that I'm already out of the house has set off a few alarm bells.

Still don't want to talk to you, I think. I'm about to throw my phone back into my bag when Spencer texts me. Now, him I definitely want to talk to. I automatically start to smile, a Pavlovian response to just seeing his name light up my screen. Mood=lifted.

How'd you do on the bio quiz?

Okay, so it's not exactly a declaration of his feelings, but still. He's checking in. That has to count for something, right?

Also, what bio quiz???

I grimace. Great. So while I was busy helping exorcise Ms. C, I missed a pop quiz in the class that is arguably my worst subject (next to geometry. And German).

I used to be a really good student. But then my mom left and I started training with Uncle Roy, and maintaining my grade point average became the least important thing in my life. I mean, it's hard to care about photosynthesis or the proper conjugation of German verbs when you're in the middle of a spiritual war.

I didn't exactly make it yesterday. I cringe even as I type the words. Spencer, of everyone, knows I can't afford to miss class. Especially bio (and geometry. And German).

It takes him a minute to respond. He's probably wondering what to say. He's so hard core about school, I'm sure he can't imagine any scenario that would cause him to miss class. And he certainly wouldn't imagine that I skipped because I was conducting an exorcism.

You okay?

I swallow. Maybe I should just tell him. I mean, what's the worst that can happen?

But I know from the way my legs have lost all feeling that I don't have the nerve. Because what if he freaks out? What if he no longer wants anything to do with me?

I can't risk it. Not yet.

All good! I even add a happy-face emoji to really throw him offtrack. *You're up early.* It's barely 8:30 a.m.

Just as I've sent the text, I get another call from Uncle Roy. I'll have to deal with him at some point, obviously, but I'm just not ready to talk to him yet.

Lacrosse practice. Gotta run. See you later?

My shoulders sag. Spencer and I literally just started texting and he's already rushing off. Why do I keep trying to make a relationship happen when he's clearly not that into it?

But a second later he sends me a rose emoji, and my mood is on the upswing again.

Oh my God. He sent me a virtual flower! I am smiling so hard, my cheeks hurt. He could have sent me a tulip or a sunflower, but he sent me a red rose! And everyone knows that red roses are a sign of love.

Before I can talk myself out of it, I shoot him the smiley face with heart eyes. Communicating my feelings through emojis isn't as scary as using actual words. Now, if only they had an emoji for *exorcist.* . . .

✖ ✖

Vanessa's sister, Isabelle, is at the kitchen table working on some kind of craft project when I barge through the O'Malleys' back door twenty minutes later. The table is covered in balls of brown and white wool.

"She's still sleeping," Izzy says, winding a long string of brown wool around a piece of cardboard.

"But it's nine o'clock." Vanessa's mom never lets anyone sleep past eight.

"My parents are in San Francisco visiting Frank," she says. "They left Antonio in charge, and he doesn't care if she stays in bed all day." Frank and Antonio are Izzy's older brothers. Antonio is taking a gap year, which mostly seems to involve playing video games and fighting with his sisters. Frank, his twin brother, is studying botany at the University of San Francisco.

"What's up with your shoes?" Izzy says, snickering.

"Quiet, you," I say, setting the box of doughnuts I brought from the shop on the table amid a sea of pom-poms. I'm still buzzing from my text exchange with Spencer. "What are you making?"

"Hedgehogs." Izzy holds up a fuzzy brown ball the size of her fist. She's painstakingly glued on googly eyes and a tiny black felt nose. It's pretty much the cutest thing I've ever seen. "I'm going to make them into keychains and sell them at the church craft sale. I have to make sixty of them by tomorrow." She scowls at the small pile of finished hedgehogs. "Vanessa's supposed to be helping me."

"I'll help you," I say.

"Really?" Izzy looks so thankful when the truth is, she's the one doing me a favor—I need to do something to take my mind off my mom. Making adorable pom-pom hedgehogs might do the trick.

She patiently demonstrates how to make a pom-pom, expertly twisting the wool around the cardboard circle. Izzy isn't much of a talker, so after she's satisfied that I'm doing a decent-enough job, we work mostly in silence. My fingers are starting to cramp when we hear someone bounding down the stairs forty-five minutes later.

Izzy's face tightens as Vanessa comes into the kitchen. She's wearing a pink T-shirt and yoga pants, her dark hair twisted into a messy topknot. She does a double take when she sees me sitting at the kitchen table with her sister.

"Hey. I didn't know you were coming over. How long have you been here?"

"Awhile," I say.

"Oooh, doughnuts." Vanessa flips the pink cardboard box open. She grabs an apple fritter and settles into the chair across from me. "Iz, I said I'd help you with these later," she says, surveying the mountain of pom-poms we've created.

Izzy scowls at her. "No need," she says, picking up the glue gun. "We're almost done."

"Oh, good." Vanessa smiles at me. "What are you doing here so early, anyway?" She takes a huge bite out of her doughnut.

I can't tell her the truth, but Vanessa can always tell when I'm lying, so I say, "I thought maybe we could go to the flea market." My mom used to take us all the time. I know it's a long shot, but I'm hoping that if I look in some of the places she used to go, I'll find her. The flea market is as good a place to start as any.

I don't know what I'll do if I do find my mom—especially if Vanessa is with me—but I'll worry about that if it happens.

"Can I come?" Izzy is carefully squirting a small blob of glue on to the back of a googly eye.

"Sure," I say.

Vanessa shoots me an annoyed look, but I don't see the harm in bringing Izzy with us. Vanessa sighs and stands up. "Just give me a few minutes to get ready."

✗ ✗

The three of us wander around the flea market for a couple of hours. Vanessa almost dies with laughter when she catches sight of the gardening clogs I'm wearing. She buys a mood ring, and Izzy buys a bunch of craft supplies, and we eat pierogi drowning in sour cream. But I can't relax or have fun because I'm slammed with memories of my mom and the thousands of times we came here together.

There's no sign of her, and yet she's everywhere I look.

✗ ✗

When I finally return home, Uncle Roy is in the kitchen, standing in front of a tabletop easel. He's gently swirling a paintbrush dripping with yellow paint around the center of the canvas.

"Is your phone broken?" he says, standing back to survey whatever it is he's trying to create. From this angle, it looks like a misshapen yellow ball. "I called you several times."

I shrug. "Sorry. Ringer was off."

I need to make him understand that the only way to get my mom back is if we work together. I need him to agree to let me help him, so I can't go all medieval on his ass for keeping this news from me, as much as I'd like to. I have to play this exactly right, calm and cool, or he will shut me down.

I take a deep breath and pull open the fridge. I grab a bottle of kombucha and pour him a glass.

"What's up with all the flowers, anyway?" I set the glass in front of him.

"In the Victorian era, flowers were used to convey messages," he says. "The daffodil"—he gestures at the yellow blob with his paintbrush—"represents hope."

"What do the other flowers you've painted represent?"

He sets his paintbrush down and picks up the glass. "Perseverance. Courage. Protection." He takes a swallow of his drink, and his whole face collapses in on itself. "What," he says, wrinkling his nose, "is this?"

"Kombucha."

"And what is kombucha?"

"Fermented tea, essentially."

"It's terrible."

"Terribly good for you," I say. "It'll help with your digestion."

"I don't need any help with my digestion," he says, handing me the glass with a scowl. His eyes finally meet mine, and his eyebrows raise in alarm. "Shelby, you look awful. Are you feeling all right?"

"I've been better." I pull my mom's file out of my bag and set it on the table, and we both stare at it, waiting for the other to break the silence.

The sigh that finally escapes from Uncle Roy sounds like steam coming from a tea kettle. A grim expression settles over his features. "You read it, I assume," he says.

I nod. I read it so many times, I practically have it memorized. And I made a copy, so I can go back to it whenever I need to. But I'm not about to tell him that.

Uncle Roy's eyes briefly drift shut. When he opens them and looks at me again, I see the toll that holding in this secret has taken on him. But whatever his reason is for keeping this from me, I already know it's not going to be good enough. Nothing he can say can make up for lying to me about my mom.

I'm suddenly like a volcano about to erupt. A vein in my forehead begins to pulse. I'm clenching my teeth together so hard, it's a miracle they don't crack. I cross my arms to keep my hands from grabbing something and throwing it across the room.

Keep calm. Don't freak out. Remember: You need him to agree to let you help.

"I'm sure you have questions," he says.

Oh, I have plenty of them. But let's start with "Why didn't you tell me?" This comes out as a yell, because the volcano cannot be contained.

"I thought maybe it would be better, easier, for you if you didn't know the truth." Uncle Roy runs his fingers over the report, smoothing the pages in a way I imagine he's probably done a thousand times before. "In the beginning, I figured I could bring her back quickly. I never expected it to take this long. Or to be this difficult." He gives me a tiny smile. "Shelby, this may surprise you, but I don't have the answers to everything. And while my intentions were good, I see now that keeping this from you was not the best idea."

It's superweird to hear Uncle Roy admit that he's wrong about something. He's always so infuriatingly sure of himself.

Knowing what happened to her isn't easy, but it's better than thinking she took off without a backward glance, with no thought of me. I feel guilty for believing that she would ever abandon me.

"I am very sorry," he says. "I hope that you can forgive me."

I get that he was trying to protect me, but I can't let him off the hook so easily. He knew I blamed myself for her leaving.

"You told me she was in Rome training at some top secret school for exorcists." So top secret that even Google couldn't turn it up. I know; I tried to find it many times.

He shifts uncomfortably. "Yes, well. The school *does* exist, but Robin has never been there," he says. "As you'll know from the file, she's still in Seattle. At least, she was up until three weeks ago."

I am trying to tamp down my fury. It's probably best if we don't talk about how he lied to me right now. I need to focus on moving forward.

"I think I've figured out a way that we can get her back," I say.

Uncle Roy shakes his head. "I can't let you be a part of this; it's much too dangerous. Your mother would not want—"

"You can't even get near her," I interrupt him. "But I can. She'll let me get close to her." She may be possessed, but she's still my mom. Some part of her will recognize me. I'm sure of it.

He gives me a look filled with such sadness that tears sting my eyes. "That has occurred to me. It's part of why I've pushed you so hard to train all these months. But this demon . . . it's unlike anything I've ever seen before. I fear . . ."

"What?"

"I fear that there isn't anything left of her to save."

My stomach drops. I think of what happened to poor Peter Satterley, how he's now a living zombie. That can't happen to my mom.

"Shelby, I know this isn't what you want to hear, but I've tried to exorcise this demon a number of times. It's much more powerful than I am," he says wearily. "And it's had a hold on Robin for too long."

"She's still in there. I know she is." She has to be. "You can't just give up on her!"

"I'm not giving up on her. I won't ever stop trying to save her. But I'm not as young as I used to be," he says. "I can't promise you that I can bring her back."

"Then let me help you! We can do it together."

But he's already shaking his head before I even finish the sentence. "I'm sorry, Shelby. What happened to your mom . . . I can't risk that happening to you, too. Robin would never forgive me if I put you in danger."

"You put me in danger all the time. How is this different from any other exorcism?"

"It's very different," he says. "You're personally involved."

"So are you!"

Uncle Roy's mouth purses. "The answer is still no."

"Come on! I have been training for almost six months. I'm ready."

"Shelby," he says. "This is not up for discussion." What he doesn't say but I hear is that he doesn't think I'm good enough. He doesn't believe I can save her.

I grab my bag and stalk out of the kitchen in a huff. I'm so tired of all his rules, of how he determines what I can and cannot do, how he refuses to listen to reason. It's his way or no way, and I'm so done with it.

✗ ✗

I spend the rest of the day wandering around Belltown, the last place, according to Uncle Roy's report, that my mom was seen. I've brought my holy water and crucifix just in case, even though I know that the chances of bumping into her are infinitesimal. She's probably long gone from this area. She might not even be in Seattle anymore.

Eventually I get tired of walking around. When I get a text from Vanessa asking if I'll meet her at a tattoo parlor in Capitol Hill, I take it as a sign that I should give up for the day—my mom would definitely want me to stop my best friend from doing something stupid.

I stand at the bus stop in front of a boutique near the

Space Needle. I watch a woman in the window slide a gauzy white peasant blouse onto a mannequin. She leaves the window but returns a minute later with a long green cardigan. I watch her dress the mannequin, her slender fingers doing up the tarnished gold buttons. It reminds me of the way my mom used to dress me when I was little, the feel of her soft hands helping me put on my jacket. My throat starts to ache.

My eyes are stinging. How could I have just accepted that she left? Why didn't I push Uncle Roy harder for the truth?

And the worst part is that I know he's right. Even if I find her, it's a long shot that I can help her. Whatever demon has its grip on my mom, it's strong enough to have kept her away from me. After so many months, her spirit will have been pushed deep, deep down. If I actually succeed in expelling the demon, there might not be anything of my mom's spirit left.

As the bus rumbles to a stop in front of me, I wipe away my tears with the sleeve of my jacket. I know what Uncle Roy says is true—that my mom would not want me to risk my soul to save her. But I also know that there's no way I won't try.

Chapter

12

"ARE YOU sure about this?" I ask Vanessa as she's about to pull open the heavy glass door to the tattoo parlor.

"For the billionth time, yes," she replies. "It's not a big deal, Shelbs. It's just a little piercing."

"It's a *tongue* piercing. And when your parents see it, they're going to ground you forever." The O'Malleys are hardcore-Catholic strict. Vanessa's curfew is eight o'clock— no jokes. They don't like her talking to any boy who isn't connected to her by blood. They are definitely not going to be down with a tongue piercing.

"It's just a tiny one. They probably won't even notice," she says. "Besides, I don't need their permission. I'm sixteen. And it's my body."

Her parents *will* notice, but there's no point arguing with her when she's clearly made up her mind. The bell above the door rings as we enter the Ink Factory, a small, cozy shop with hardwood floors and exposed brick walls. A couple of reclining black leather chairs, almost like what you'd see in a dentist's office, are parked in front of tall, gold-framed mirrors. The front counter is made of amber glass blocks with a polished granite top. The place smells faintly of antiseptic.

The guy standing behind the counter glances at us, and my heart stops. He looks very familiar. Like an older, heavily tattooed version of Spencer. He's Spencer with five years of hard partying under his belt.

"Hey, don't you think that guy looks like Spencer?" I whisper.

Vanessa has zero chill, and she openly gives the guy the once-over. "Practically identical. But they're brothers, so I guess that makes sense," she says, making no effort to lower her voice.

All the blood drains from my face. I grab her elbow. "What?"

"I might have mentioned to Spencer that I wanted to get a piercing," Vanessa says, carefully removing my claws from her arm. "And he might have mentioned that this is his brother's shop. He said he'd meet us here."

I feel a flush rise through me. Butterflies immediately take flight in my stomach. When I sent him that heart-eyes emoji this morning, I thought I'd have a bit more time before I saw him again.

"Why didn't you warn me?" My voice sounds unnaturally high. She could have at least given me a heads-up. I would have dashed home to change out of my threadbare jeans and ancient T-shirt. At the very least, I would have brushed my hair!

"Because I knew you would freak out and get all obsessive," she says. "I wanted to spare you the angst."

"I'm not angsty." I expect to see Spencer at school, but having him sprung on me in the wild, when I'm not prepared, has my entire body vibrating with nerves.

Vanessa snorts. "Please. Shelby, you need to learn to relax. He's just a boy."

The guy—Spencer's brother, Mark—is flipping through a thick blue binder, but I'm certain he's only pretending to be busy to spare me the humiliation of knowing that he's heard every word. He's wearing a long-sleeve white T-shirt, his dark hair swept back from his forehead with a red bandana. Just behind him, lying on a fluffy purple cushion, is a massive black Rottweiler. The dog starts to growl as we walk toward the counter.

"Cerberus, knock it off," Mark says, shaking his head. "Sorry. He's usually pretty friendly."

That dog looks the opposite of friendly. He looks like he would happily make a meal of us. Also, I'm pretty sure Cerberus is the name of the three-headed dog that guards the gates of the underworld. Which seems fitting.

Mark flips the binder closed. "How can I help you ladies?"

"I want to get my tongue pierced," Vanessa says.

"How old are you?"

"Sixteen."

He nods. "All right then." He hands her a consent form, and Vanessa scribbles her signature, then slides it back across the counter. While Mark goes over the logistics of what he's about to do to her tongue, I look around at the different-size picture frames covering the walls. The frames showcase a bunch of tattoo options, everything from skulls and crossbones and four-leaf clovers to big red hearts. One tattoo in particular catches my eye—it looks kind of like a bar code, but instead of a bunch of different numbers, there are only sixes—666, to be precise.

The number of the beast.

I glance uneasily at Spencer's brother. He's leading

Vanessa over to one of the leather chairs. Mark sits on a rolling stool in front of Vanessa, so they're eye level, and slides on a pair of rubber gloves. "Okay, let's see what we're working with," he says. Vanessa sticks out her tongue, and he grasps it between two fingers and leans forward, lifting it up to check for I-don't-know-what. Then he grabs a marker and draws a small dot in the center of her tongue.

Mark picks up something that looks like a pair of salad tongs and squeezes Vanessa's tongue with it. He holds up a long needle and says, "Hold still. You're going to feel a little pinch."

This is when things start to get a little fuzzy. I'm suddenly sweaty, and my legs feel like they're not strong enough to support me. I slouch against the wall.

"You all right?" Mark asks, glancing at me.

"I'm fine."

Why did I just tell him that I'm fine? I'm not fine at all. The room is dim, like someone just turned down the lights.

"You might want to sit down," he says. "Put your head between your knees."

Good idea.

I drop into the chair next to Vanessa and bend over at the waist, letting my hair graze the floor. My vision slowly starts to return.

"Deep breath." I'm not sure if he's talking to me or

Vanessa. A second later, I hear her grunt, and Mark says, "All done. You're a champ." I hear the castors on the stool roll as he stands up. "I'm going to get you some ice to help with the swelling." He pats my back and says, "I'll get some for you as well." His footsteps cross the store and disappear into another room.

Vanessa glances at me, her eyebrows raised. "Tho othay?"

"I'm fine." I sit up slowly, feeling ridiculous. I can face down a demon with no problem, but I almost faint at the sight of a needle? Pathetic.

She stands up to check out her piercing in the thick-framed gold mirror hanging on the wall. She sticks her tongue out to show me the tiny silver ball.

"Cool."

Vanessa shifts her gaze to the doorway Mark went through. "He's cute, right?" she asks. Her words still sound a bit garbled, and I can hear the ball click against her teeth.

I know where she's going with this, and I need to head her off at the pass. "Sure. But he's also, like, way old."

"He's not that old."

"Vanessa, he's at least five years older than we are," I say.

"Five years is nothing."

"Tell that to the judge."

She swats me on the arm. The bell over the door rings, and Spencer walks in just as Mark returns with two cups of ice. I'm used to seeing Spencer in his Catholic uniform, but he's even hotter in jeans and a T-shirt. I don't think I've ever seen him in short sleeves, and the sight of his bare arms, his just-the-right-amount-of-muscles, gives me all sorts of dirty thoughts. He glances at me, and I'm sure he can probably see the cartoon hearts in my real eyes.

"Little brother," Mark says. "What's up? Didn't know you were coming by."

"Came to see these two," Spencer says.

Mark gives me a wide smile. "Ah, you must be Shelby, then."

I smile back at him. He knows my name, so clearly Spencer has mentioned me. A good sign.

He hands me a red solo cup of ice. "You all right now?"

"What happened?" Spencer asks.

"She was just feeling a little faint," he says as I shake a piece of ice out of the cup and put it against my forehead. "Nothing to be embarrassed about. Spence here can relate, can't you, bro?" He grins. "Fainted dead away when I tried to pierce his ear last year."

Spencer shakes his head. "Not a story I'm excited you're sharing."

"Oh, come on," Mark says. "We're all friends here."

Vanessa laughs, like he's just said something extraordinarily witty. She tucks one long black curl behind her ear, and she actually bats her eyelashes. It's the most super-obvious display of flirting ever, and Mark doesn't even notice. I inwardly cringe because I know his obliviousness will just make her want him more.

He turns to me. "So, Shelby. I'm having a party next Friday," he says. "You should come. Keep my little brother company."

Before I can answer, Vanessa says, "We're in."

"See, little bro? That's how you ask a girl out." He chuckles and punches Spencer in the shoulder.

"Smooth, Mark. Thanks," Spencer says, rubbing his shoulder.

Mark winks at me. He gestures for Vanessa to follow him up to the counter so she can pay for her piercing.

Spencer scrubs a hand through his thick, dark hair. "So that didn't exactly go as I planned."

"It's okay," I say.

"No, it's really not. But I'll wait until you've left before I murder him." He gives me a half-smile. "I was going to ask you to come myself. I would have worked up the nerve eventually."

I smile back at him. I'm not totally sure this is a date—for all I know he's asked half of St. Joseph's to come to this party. But, aside from the time Spencer drove me home, we've never hung out outside of school before. A party is a lot less pressure than a date, and it's a good way for us to get to know each other better.

"So you'll come?" He rubs the back of his neck. He usually has such a tight hold on himself, so seeing him so nervous makes something bloom inside my chest.

"Wouldn't miss it," I say.

I am in danger of falling very hard for Spencer Callaghan.

Chapter

13

VANESSA'S PARENTS made her take out her tongue piercing, because of course they did. They also grounded her, but she somehow managed to convince them to let her stay over at my house this weekend, although she held back the part about going to a party. I guess her parents figure she can't get up to much trouble staying over in the home of a priest, but what they don't realize is that Uncle Roy is not a prison guard; he pretty much lets me come and go as I please.

"So did you ask Spencer if Mark's single?" Vanessa says, sliding on her purple aviator sunglasses. We're sitting on the school steps, the remains of our lunch littered around us.

"No, but I did find out that he's twenty-three," I say. "I'm pretty sure that if you got together, your parents would have him arrested."

"What are you going to wear to the party tonight?" Vanessa's trick when she's presented with something she doesn't want to hear is to change the subject.

"I haven't thought about it." I don't have a lot to pick from. Uncle Roy isn't cheap, exactly, but he's not down with paying for anything that he believes costs more than it should. And never is this more evident than when I have to buy clothes. He gives me some money to compensate for the time my exorcism training eats up—time I could be spending at a part-time job to earn money that I could use for a decent pair of jeans—but trust me when I say that his stipend doesn't get me very far.

"Maybe I should just wear this," Vanessa says, smoothing her kilt over her knees. "Aren't most guys into the Catholic school girl look?"

"Ew," I say.

Vanessa laughs, even though I totally wasn't kidding. And I'm not sure she was, either.

"Maybe I should get a tattoo," she says. "Somewhere my

parents won't see it. A four-leaf clover would be cute, don't you think?"

"What is up with all the rebellion lately?"

Her parents are strict, sure, but what Vanessa doesn't seem to get is that the more she acts out, the more their grip tightens.

"I just want to do me," she says, leaning back on her elbows. "What's wrong with that?"

"Nothing. But can't you do you without getting a tattoo?"

"Nope."

I feel a wrench in my chest. All this talk of parents just reminds me that mine aren't around. And, okay, my mom has a pretty solid excuse for not being here, but I've been carrying the guilt for what happened that night for five months.

"You okay?" Vanessa asks, nudging me with her foot.

No. But I give her a small smile. "Just thinking that if you're going to get a tattoo, a four-leaf clover is perfect," I say. "Because if your parents find out that you got one, you're going to need all the luck you can get."

Chapter

14

SPENCER'S BROTHER lives in the middle of nowhere in a rundown cabin almost completely hidden by trees. I park Uncle Roy's car in a grass field, and Vanessa and I walk toward the house.

Classic rock is playing from behind the log walls so loudly that the front door is thumping like a beating heart. The unmistakable smell of weed drifts on the chilly night air. Vanessa curses with each step as her neon yellow heels sink into the grass. She's not used to wearing heels, so she looks a bit like a baby giraffe that's just learning to walk. The shoes, coupled with her jeans, were carefully selected to make Mark notice her. Her hair is long and loose, her dark curls turned up at such full volume that they're practically shouting.

We step onto the porch. I knock on the door, which is painted a soft blue-green. I knock a little harder, and someone turns the music down. A few seconds later, a short man with long, out-of-control curly gray hair—not unlike Vanessa's own wild hairstyle—answers. He's older, approaching Uncle Roy's age bracket, and built like a teapot, round in the middle. Black leather suspenders with skulls imprinted on them are holding up his faded black jeans, and he's wearing scuffed motorcycle boots.

"Hi. Um, is Spencer here?"

A smile crawls across the man's face. Friendly or creepy, I'm not exactly sure, but I'm going to take it as a good sign that he's opened the door to let us inside. Either Spencer is here, or this guy is inviting us in so he can kill us.

Hopefully Spencer is here.

We scoot past him. The door closes behind us, and the man grunts and lumbers over to a table in the center of a huge room where a good-looking blond guy and a woman about my mom's age are playing cards. The woman has a huge stack of poker chips in front of her, while the blond guy has a sour look on his face. Mark's friends, I assume.

"Shelby!"

I turn around and, speak of the devil, there's Mark parked in front of a massive stone fireplace. He's holding on to the collar of a big black Rottweiler, the same dog that was at the tattoo shop. It starts to growl when I approach.

Seriously, what is up with this dog?

"Hi," I say.

"Good to see you." Mark strokes the dog's fur, and the animal stops growling and puddles at his feet, his long, pink tongue curling out of his mouth. "Veronica, right?" he asks Vanessa.

The smile freezes on her face. It's not a great sign that he doesn't remember her name. "Vanessa."

"Right. Knew it started with a *V*," he says. "How's your tongue? Healing all right?"

"Your place is nice," I say to save Vanessa from having to explain that her parents made her take the piercing out. I know she doesn't want Mark to think that she even has parents, because then he might remember that she's only sixteen and not an appropriate person for him to date.

"It belongs to my uncle. I'm just crashing here for a while. Looking after Cerberus while he's out of town," he says, scratching the dog behind the ears.

Cerberus. Right. The devil's dog.

"What's with the blue ceiling?" Vanessa asks. I glance up. The ceiling is painted the same blue-green as the door. It's out of place with the rest of the cabin, which looks like it hasn't seen much in the way of improvement in generations.

Before Mark can answer, a tall, red-haired girl appears holding two red solo cups. He shifts so she can sit down beside him. Vanessa visibly deflates as the girl puts a proprietary hand on his thigh. When he takes the cup from her, the sleeve of his plaid shirt slides down his arm just enough to reveal a small tattoo on the inside of his wrist.

666.

The sign of the beast.

My stomach drops. Why does Mark have that tattoo?

He catches me staring and yanks his sleeve down. "Spence is in the back room," he says. He's smiling, but I know a dismissal when I hear one. For whatever reason, Mark doesn't like that I know he has that tattoo.

I smile back, hoping it's sincere enough to convince him that I had no idea what I was looking at. But I'm not a very good actress. And he's not an idiot.

My mind is reeling as Vanessa and I head down the hall. There doesn't seem to be an evil presence in this house. And Mark doesn't give off a demon vibe; he doesn't smell like rotten eggs and his eyes are a clear blue. I'm sure he's not possessed.

Pretty sure.

But the fact that he has that tattoo and that he clearly didn't want me to see it is weird. It means something. I'm just not sure what.

"Let's just say hi to Spencer and then get the hell out of here," Vanessa says, stopping to kick off her heels.

I'm not surprised she wants to leave, but I'm hoping her mood will turn around. This is my opportunity to move my relationship with Spencer past emojis and to the next level.

We enter a small room with rough wood walls. Spencer's standing with his back to us, facing a dart board that's mounted on one wall, about to throw a dart at his friend Grayson's head.

"Vanessa," Grayson yells.

Spencer turns. "Shelby. You're here," he says. The way his voice rolls over my name causes something to flutter inside of me.

"You weren't actually going to throw that at him, were you?" I point to the dart in his hand.

He smiles, then turns back around. The dart whistles past Grayson's head and neatly lodges in the board, dangerously close to his left ear.

Grayson measures the distance between the dart and his

head. He holds his fingers up, a centimeter apart. "Sheesh, bro. That was a little too close."

"Haven't missed yet," Spencer says.

"We just came to say hi, then we're leaving," Vanessa says.

"Aw, you can't leave. You just got here." Grayson slings his arm around her shoulder. Without shoes on, she's considerably shorter than he is; her head is about level with his armpit. "At least have one drink. We have beer."

I fold my hands under my chin. Please.

Vanessa rolls her eyes. "Fine. But just one drink." She lets Grayson lead her out of the room in search of the promised keg, leaving Spencer and me alone. Well, as alone as we can be in a house full of people.

I should ask him about Mark's tattoo and why that damned dog is named Cerberus, but Spencer reaches out and laces his fingers through mine. My heart feels like it might burst.

"Come with me," he says. "I want to show you something."

He tugs me through the back door and out into the yard. My heart is beating wildly as we walk between the trees and toward a row of small cabins. He heads to the one farthest from the house. It's made of rough logs, just like the lodge, with the same blue-green door.

We go inside. The first thing I notice is the cedar smell—it's like being inside a hope chest. Spencer pulls on a chain hanging from the ceiling. The bare light bulb casts a glow of yellow light over the room. The cabin is empty aside from a scarred wooden desk covered in various tools, some loose black stones, and ropes of silver chain.

"My uncle lets me use this place as my studio," Spencer says as I walk over to the desk.

I pick up a hammered copper bracelet. "You make jewelry."

He nods and hands me a square black stone on a thin chain. I know that bringing me here is his way of letting me see him, a way to show me who he is.

"It's beautiful." The stone is smooth and flat. I run my finger over the two circles engraved on the top. "What does this mean?"

"It's an old Gaelic protection symbol."

"You know Gaelic?"

"Not even a little," he says. "But I know how to google."

"What does it offer protection from, exactly?"

"Evil spirits, if you believe in them," he says with a half-smile. "I just like the look of it."

"It does look pretty badass," I say. "How did you learn to make these?"

He shrugs. "My dad's a silversmith. Sometimes he uses black onyx."

"I thought your dad was a professor."

"He is. But he used to make jewelry. When he quit, he gave me all his tools." Spencer clears his throat. "That one's for you."

My breath catches. I can't believe he made this for me. If I needed another sign that he likes me, that his feelings run deeper than friendship, then he's just given it to me. And as happy as that makes me, I also feel guilty. I still haven't told him I'm an exorcist, and he deserves to know who he's getting involved with.

I have to tell him before this goes any further. But the words stick in my throat and I start to shake. I'm so afraid that he's going to freak out, that it will change the way he feels about me. I've waited so long for this moment, and I don't want to ruin it.

So, like a coward, I don't say anything. I let him take the rune and move behind me. I lift my hair, and his fingers whisper against the back of my neck as he fastens the necklace. The rune nestles just above my heart. His fingers linger on my skin, sending major electric shocks through my body.

My heart is pounding so hard, I'm sure it's going to punch

right through my chest. This is the moment. When I turn around, he's going to kiss me. Or I'm going to kiss him. Either way, we're going to be kissing.

All I need to do is turn around.

And I've just about gathered the courage when someone knocks on the cabin door. Before Spencer even has the chance to ask who it is, the blond guy I saw playing poker when I first arrived barges in. He's about my height, and his hair is so blond, it's almost transparent.

"Sorry to interrupt," he says, but from the intense look on his face, I can tell that he's not sorry at all. "Can I talk to you for a second?" he asks Spencer.

Spencer sighs. "Shelby, this is Lucas. Lucas, Shelby."

The guy that called him when we were in the library.

Lucas gives me a cursory glance, frowning when his dark eyes land on the rune around my neck. He turns back to Spencer. "This is important."

Hello? What he's interrupting is important!

But instead of demanding that Lucas leaves, Spencer says, "Fine." He touches my arm. "I'll meet you back at the house?"

Whatever. The moment is lost—probably forever—so fine. I'll go. But I'm not going to pretend to be happy about it.

I slam the cabin door. I hear them whispering furiously as I hurry back across the yard, toward the main house. Vanessa and Grayson are sitting on the back steps, facing each other, a board game spread out between them. They're so focused on the game that they don't even look up as I approach.

Vanessa's wearing Grayson's hoodie. Her hair has grown wilder, like someone has messed it up, and from the goofy smile on Grayson's face, I know that Vanessa has been too busy with him to wonder what was taking me so long.

Busy playing with the Ouija board.

What is she doing? Ouija boards are portals from the underworld. These two are just asking to be possessed.

"Where did you find that?" I ask.

"In one of the bedrooms upstairs," Grayson replies without taking his eyes off the game.

Vanessa's fingers are resting on the little plastic planchette. "It wasn't working in the house for some reason. I thought it might help if we brought it out here."

The planchette starts to glide across the board, picking up speed as it moves through the alphabet. *A B C D E F . . .*

"You're moving it again, right?" Grayson asks nervously as the planchette stops on *G.*

Vanessa just smiles. Maybe she's just screwing with him.

Please let her just be screwing with him.

Grayson lifts his fingers off the planchette. The plastic piece keeps zipping around the board, even though Vanessa's fingers are barely touching it. It's moving too fast now for me to read what it's spelling out, but Vanessa seems to have no problem deciphering the message. Whatever it is, it makes her smile widen.

"Vanessa, we need to get going," I say.

Vanessa shakes her head. "I'm almost done."

I dig in my bag for Uncle Roy's car keys. I lean toward her and shine the tiny flashlight attached to the key ring right in her eyes.

"What the hell?" Vanessa's hands fly up to cover her face, breaking her connection with the Ouija board. But I see her eyes—still a familiar, clear blue—and relief floods through me.

I click off the light. "All good."

The two of them are staring at me. An explanation is obviously required.

"Just . . . checking to see if you're okay to drive," I say.

"I guess that would make sense if I had my license," Vanessa says. "Why are you being crazy?"

"It was a joke. Obviously I know you can't drive. Ha-ha." I clear my throat. "Um, we really do need to go."

"Okay, okay," Vanessa says.

Grayson extends his hand to help her up just as Spencer walks across the grass, Lucas trailing a few feet behind him. Whatever just went down between them in the cabin wasn't good; neither of them looks happy. So that makes three of us.

Lucas ignores us as he walks up the porch steps and into the house. The screen door bangs shut behind him.

"Yikes," Vanessa says. "What's his problem?"

Spencer shakes his head. "Difference of opinion."

"Well. We really should get going," I say.

"Just give us one more minute," Vanessa says, pulling Grayson into the shadows at the other end of the porch. The shadows can't hide the slurping sound of their kissing, however. It's unbearably awkward and a painful reminder of what Spencer and I didn't get to do in his workshop.

Spencer rubs his hand against the back of his neck. "Sorry about Lucas. Once he gets his mind set on something, he doesn't back down."

"Must have been important."

He nods. "It was. But his timing could have been better."

The heavy feeling in my chest lifts a little. He's not happy that we were interrupted, either. But he's also not giving me any details on what they fought about. He's so guarded.

I glance down at the abandoned Ouija board near my feet. I don't want to touch it, but I can't just leave it out here for anyone to stumble across. The best way to get rid of a Ouija board is to sprinkle it with salt, wrap it in cotton, and bury it far beneath the ground, but I'm sure Spencer will think I'm beyond weird if I suggest we lay the game to rest in his uncle's backyard.

But Spencer surprises me by pulling his sleeve over his hand and reaching down to flip the board closed, taking care that his skin doesn't come in contact with the board, as if it's made of corrosive material. He makes protective charms to ward off evil spirits, so I guess I shouldn't be surprised that he's reluctant to touch this game. He places the board and the planchette into the box, then nudges the box across the cedar deck with the toe of his boot until it's nestled under a chair, out of sight.

"I'll have Mark come and get it later," he says.

Maybe he wouldn't think it so weird if I suggest we bury it in the backyard after all.

Vanessa and Grayson emerge from the shadows. She smooths her hand over her wild hair. Grayson stumbles after her, a goofy smile on his face.

"All right, now we can go," Vanessa says, leaning down to grab her shoes from the deck. She hooks her arm around me and tugs me into the house. I glance over my shoulder at Spencer, but he's already walking back toward his cabin. From the slump of his shoulders, it's clear that I'm not the only one who's disappointed with how this evening turned out.

Chapter

15

WHEN I wake up the next morning, Vanessa's sitting on the air mattress on my bedroom floor, *The History of Exorcism* spread open in her lap. "What is this?" she asks.

My stomach plunges. Uncle Roy insisted that I read this impossibly thick, densely written, incredibly old book that traces exorcism through the ages. The guy who wrote it is supposedly some expert on the Catholic religion at NYU.

I definitely don't want her to know the real reason I have that book.

"Oh. I found it in the church library," I say, sitting up in bed. "I thought it looked interesting."

Vanessa raises an eyebrow like she doesn't quite believe me and slides the book back under my bed without further comment. I should probably ask her why she's looking through my stuff, but I'm just grateful she didn't find Mom's file. I wouldn't know how to begin to explain that.

"So. You and Grayson?" The quickest way to throw her offcourse is to ask her about Grayson O'Neill.

She wrinkles her nose. "I had a weak moment."

"He's a good guy. I get why you like him."

"I don't *like* him. He's too goofy. And way too young." But I can tell she's fighting a smile.

"Vanessa, he's only a year younger than we are. There's a much bigger age difference between you and Mark." Not that she and Mark are ever going to happen. After last night, I think she's finally given up on that idea.

She shakes her head. "I was just messing around," she says. "Nothing's going to come of it."

"Speaking of messing around. What was up with the Ouija board?"

"Trying to ask the spirits some questions, natch. Isn't that the whole purpose of a Ouija board?"

"You really shouldn't play around with that thing," I say. "It's evil."

Vanessa snorts. "Says the girl who's reading up on exorcisms for fun." She climbs off the air mattress and stretches into warrior pose, then moves smoothly into downward-facing dog.

"So what did you ask it?"

She glances up at me through a curtain of dark hair. "I wanted to know who I'm going to hook up with."

I smile. She doesn't need a Ouija board to tell her that—the answer is fairly obvious, even if she refuses to admit it.

"You want some breakfast?"

"Yes," she says. "But can you go get it? Bring it in here?"

One of these days she's going to have to get over her fear of Uncle Roy. "Vanessa, he knows you slept over," I say. "You can't avoid him all morning. You will have to leave my room at some point."

"I'm not dressed," she says, lying down on the floor and raising her legs in the air. Her cartoon sheep–covered pajamas slide down her calves. "I can't talk to a priest in my pajamas."

"I talk to him in mine all the time."

"He makes me nervous," she says. "He has this intense way of looking at me. . . . It's like he can see inside my brain. And trust me, the last thing I want is for Father Roy to know what I'm thinking about. Because if he did, I'm pretty sure I'd have to spend the rest of my life in confession."

I soften. I know that feeling all too well.

"All right, fine. What do you want? Pancakes? Oatmeal?"

She lowers her legs and extends her arms, splayed out like a starfish. "Do you have any Pop-Tarts?"

"I think I have a few left," I say, throwing off the covers and getting out of bed. I keep an emergency stash of junk food in a shoebox at the back of my closet, hidden from Uncle Roy.

But apparently not hidden well enough, because when I pick it up, the box is suspiciously light. I remove the lid and peer inside, but instead of Pop-Tarts and chocolate bars, all that's left is a package of red licorice.

Uncle Roy hates red licorice.

I toss the bag at Vanessa. "I'll make us some oatmeal."

✗ ✗

An hour later, after Vanessa sneaks out of the house through my bedroom window, I head to the rectory. Uncle Roy's sitting at his desk, working on his sermon. Or thinking about it anyway; he's leaning back in his chair, chewing on the stem of his glasses.

I set an extra-large kale smoothie down in front of him.

I'm still mad at him, but I'm set on trying to convince him to let me help.

His mouth purses, and he pushes the glass away. "Thank you, but I'm not hungry."

"That's probably because you filled up on Pop-Tarts," I say, moving the glass back toward him.

He pretends not to hear me. But after a solid minute of staring at him, he concedes and takes a small sip of the smoothie. He grimaces but doesn't spit it out. Progress!

I sit down at my desk across from him and start to rummage through all the junk in the top drawer, of which there is plenty. This desk used to belong to my mom. She was—is—exceedingly neat, and she'd be appalled if she saw the state it's been reduced to: a million pens, candy bar wrappers, the pink rhinestone ear buds I've been looking for everywhere. And underneath all the detritus, stuck to the bottom of the drawer: a photo of us.

I gently pry the photo off the wood. I remember when this picture was taken—we were in Maine, the summer after my dad left. My mom and I are standing in front of the belly of a tall white lighthouse. The lighthouse is perched on a rocky cliff facing the stormy gray ocean. It was a blow-your-skirt-up windy kind of day, and the spray from the ocean misted my face as we leaned against the rough stone building.

My mom had one arm firmly wrapped around my shoulders, while her other hand tried to corral her dark hair to keep it from blowing into her eyes.

If the current situation were reversed—if I were possessed—my mom would not rest until she had me back. She would do whatever it took to help me. She would never let Uncle Roy talk her out of it.

I prop the photo up against the pen holder on my desk. "I've been thinking . . ." I say.

"Mmhm." He's bent over his leather journal, his fountain pen moving smoothly across the page.

"You have to let me help you find my mom."

Uncle Roy glances at me warily. "Shelby, we've been through this."

"You've been through this," I say. "I never said I agreed."

He closes his eyes and rubs his temples, like I've just given him a pounding headache. "I don't think you understand what's at stake here," he says. "I've tried to impress upon you just how dangerous it could be if you confront your mother. It could be dangerous for her and, even worse, dangerous for you. You are not equipped to deal with a demon of this nature—"

"You don't think that I can do it."

"I'm not sure that *I* can do it," he says. "And I have a lifetime of experience."

"But maybe if we were working together, maybe if she saw me—"

Uncle Roy holds up his hand. "Shelby. No. I will not put you in that kind of danger."

Clearly we're at an impasse. There's nothing that I can say to convince him. When he digs his heels in about something, it's impossible to change his mind.

I scowl at him. He wants me to stay out of the way and let him handle this, but he's been handling it for five months and that's gotten him exactly nowhere.

Well, if he's not going to help me, then I'll figure out a way to do it myself.

Chapter

16

THE SEATTLE GREAT WHEEL is a giant Ferris wheel that overlooks Elliott Bay and the downtown core, depending on which way you're facing. I've never been on it—most of the people who ride it are tourists—but when Spencer texts me to ask if I want to meet him there, I tell him yes, even though I'm supposed to be training with Uncle Roy. Skipping my training session is a no-brainer, partly because I'm still mad at Uncle Roy but mostly because I really want to spend time with Spencer. Maybe this is our chance to make up for what didn't happen at the party.

Spencer's waiting for me on the boardwalk. My stomach starts to flutter. He's all windblown dark-brown hair and blue eyes crinkling at the corners, broad shoulders, and ears that stick out just enough to save him from being too perfect. Just looking at him does crazy things to me, so I can't even imagine what will happen if he kisses me. I might just spontaneously combust.

"Hey," he says, smiling. "I'm glad you could make it. I know it's pretty last-minute."

"I'm glad you texted." I smile back at him, and we stand there, just smiling at each other, until he finally reaches for my hand. My entire body lightens, and I feel as if I would float away like a balloon if he weren't holding on to me.

We join the line to embark on the ride. Spencer tucks our joined hands into the pocket of his windbreaker, and it's such a boyfriend move that my heart feels like it could burst. And then I remember: I still haven't told him that I'm an exorcist. Even worse: I'm on a date when really I should be out looking for my mom. Guilt washes over me.

I push thoughts of my mom down deep. Having fun while she's out there, God-knows-where, feels wrong, but I'm on the edge of losing my mind with worry. I've realized that until I can get Uncle Roy to agree to let me help him look for her,

I'm stuck. And I might as well be stuck with Spencer, rather than wandering aimlessly around Seattle trying to find her.

As for the fact that I haven't told Spencer I'm an exorcist yet . . . I guess there's no better time than the present.

I feel nauseous. If he doesn't understand, if he thinks I'm a total freak, then we'll be over before we really even got started. He doesn't strike me as judgmental, but still, I can't predict how he'll react.

I take a deep breath. Maybe I'm worrying for nothing. Maybe he won't care.

"Spencer?"

He looks over at me and smiles, and . . . I lose my nerve again.

I'll tell him before the end of this date.

Probably.

I crane my head back to try to see the top of the Great Wheel, but it's impossible. From this angle, the glass gondolas seem to be rising smoothly into the heavens. "Exactly how high does this thing go?"

"One hundred and seventy-five feet," Spencer says. His voice wavers slightly, and I glance over at him. Beads of sweat are starting to form on his forehead, even though it's not that warm out.

"Have you been on it before?"

He shakes his head. "I'll let you in on a secret," he says. "I'm terrified of heights."

"Um, so you want to go a million feet in the air because . . . ?"

"My brother always says the best way to get over a fear is to face it head-on," he says. His palms are sweaty, but I'm too busy being excited that Spencer wants me to be with him while he conquers his fear to be grossed out.

"I thought you could help distract me," he says. His eyes drop to my lips, and my cheeks start to flush. I read in a magazine once that when someone stares at your mouth, it's a surefire sign that they're thinking about kissing you.

Spencer is thinking about kissing me! We're going to kiss on the Great Wheel!

I am too nervous to say anything. We reach the front of the line. A girl in a black fleece jacket and navy baseball cap with the Great Wheel embroidered on it slides open the door.

Spencer swallows. For a minute I think he's going to back out, that his fear of heights is about to get the best of him, but then he gently tugs me inside.

The gondola is made completely of glass. We sit on the leather bench seat, facing the water. There's plenty of room, but we're pressed tightly against each other. He lets go of my hand and slides his arm around my shoulder. We're not even in the air yet, but my stomach is behaving as if we're doing somersaults.

And then a man climbs in with us. I frown. I'd assumed we'd have the entire gondola to ourselves, so the fact that we have to share it is a real bummer. No way am I going to make out with Spencer in front of an audience. I know it's not the man's intention to be a third wheel, but he totally is, and I can't help glaring at him.

He settles into the seat across from us. He's wearing a gray suit with a burgundy tie, like he's just left the office and decided to take a spin on the Great Wheel. As one does.

Spencer tenses beside me, so I turn my attention back to him. He's blinking rapidly, and his breathing has slowed. I think he might be on the edge of a panic attack. I'm about to ask him if he wants to get off—I'm all for facing your fears, but this doesn't seem like the best idea—when the girl slides the gondola door closed and locks us in.

And, barely one second later, the smell hits me. A terrible, unmistakable, rotten-egg smell.

I clap my hand over my nose and look at the man across from us in alarm. He's in some kind of trance, staring without really seeing. Totally creepy. His pupils are totally blown out, too, so if I had any doubts that he's possessed, his eyes have just confirmed it.

I feel a stab of fury. You've got to be kidding me. Of all the gondolas, he gets into mine? This is so unfair.

Spencer has disappeared so completely inside of himself that he doesn't seem to have noticed the appalling smell. I don't even know how that's possible—it literally smells like we're inside an anal cavity—but okay. Before I can tell him that we need to get off this thing *right now*, the gondola gracefully lifts us into the air.

Spencer's face drains of all color. He's clutching my fingers so tightly, I'm afraid he's going to grind my bones to dust.

He's already so freaked out, I can't exactly tell him that we're trapped on a Ferris wheel with a possessed person, especially when said possessed person is sitting two feet away and will likely overhear.

The Great Wheel moves smoothly upward, rising high over Elliott Bay. My mind is racing, trying to figure out how to handle this disaster. The best course of action is probably just to ignore this demon. He seems to be minding his own business, staring blankly out the window. This ride probably isn't very long, and when we get to the bottom, I can call Uncle Roy and report this guy. Let him deal with the problem.

Done and done.

In the meantime, I'll try and calm my nerves by pretending he doesn't exist. I'll just concentrate on Spencer.

"You doing okay?"

He doesn't answer me. I put my hand on his knee to stop it from jiggling. His eyes are squeezed shut, which is probably a good thing because, as it turns out, one hundred and seventy-five feet is VERY HIGH. I'm beginning to feel queasy.

"Probably best to keep your eyes closed," I tell him. For more than one reason, like I don't want him to notice that there's something really off about our travel companion.

The Wheel gets to the top and the gondola stops, gently rocking back and forth. It feels like we're floating in midair. From this height, the boats bobbing in the choppy gray-blue water far below us are the size of bathtub toys.

Unfortunately, my plan to ignore the demon across from me is about to backfire, because he seems to have come out of his trance. His face has turned a dark shade of red, and he's beginning to snort. Also, his butt is hovering a few inches off the seat, so that's just great; now he's levitating.

Crap. I'm going to have to deal with this.

Even though Spencer's eyes are still screwed tightly shut, I don't see how I'm going to be able to exorcise this guy without him catching on. He's about to find out who I really am, and I can only hope that he'll be able to deal with it.

Okay, think. I don't have my supplies with me. However,

Spencer is wearing a crucifix. I could use it to expel the demon. I mean, it's probably not any different than the one I normally use, other than that mine is blessed by Uncle Roy.

I don't want to tip the demon off, so I pretend to massage Spencer's neck. His face relaxes a tiny bit, so I feel bad when I stop rubbing a few seconds later and unclasp his necklace. His brow furrows in confusion, but he doesn't open his eyes.

The pendant is only about the size of my thumbnail, but it's still a crucifix. I close my fingers around the cross and say a quick prayer in my head that I can actually pull this exorcism off and that Spencer won't think I'm a total freak when he sees what's about to happen.

The gondola starts to move again. The man is now hovering around the ceiling—I have to start the exorcism now. Otherwise I'm going to have a hard time explaining what's going on to the Great Wheel staff when this thing is on the ground.

Okay. I can do this.

I hold the miniature crucifix out in front of me—it's so tiny, I have to pinch my fingers together to keep from dropping it. *"Deus, audi oratiónem meam; áuribus pércipe verba oris mei,"* I say, trying my best to sound confident. *"Nam supérbi insurréxerunt contra me, et violénti quæsierunt vitam meam."*

Spencer's eyes snap open. I can't look at him to see how

he's reacting to what I'm doing; I have to keep my focus on expelling this demon.

With a growl, the man drops back down into his seat. His entire body goes stiff, then begins to shake violently, as if he's being electrocuted.

Good start! The incantation seems to be working.

The man's face contorts, and he's spitting and foaming at the mouth. And then—oh Lord—his head starts to revolve on his neck, bones cracking and popping, until it twists all the way around and his face is on the wrong side of his body.

I wince. I really hate it when they do that.

"*Nam ex omni tribulatióne eripuit me, et inimícos meos confúsos vidit óculos meus!*"

The man starts to emit this high-pitched noise, almost like a siren, which echoes off the glass walls. I wrack my brain, trying to remember if Uncle Roy ever mentioned this particular ear-splitting sound and what it could possibly mean. My eardrums feel like they're about to burst.

We've gone another full rotation and are at the top of the Great Wheel again when the man finally collapses forward. His body is smoking, clouds of steam rising off of him. But fortunately his head is on the right way again, returned to its natural position.

Did I do it?

I lean cautiously toward him. He doesn't move.

I think I did it.

But I can't celebrate just yet—first I need to make sure that the demon is really gone. Except when I lean forward to give him a good poke with the tiny crucifix, the man bolts upright. He twists toward me and gives me the most gruesome smile, one that sends a snake of fear right up my spine.

"*D-deus, audi or-oratiónem meam,*" I say, stumbling over the incantation. The man just laughs and bares his teeth at me. My fingers are shaking so hard that I drop Spencer's crucifix.

Spencer. I sneak a look at him. He has a strange expression on his face, like he can't quite believe what's happening right in front of him. He reaches for my hand and squeezes my fingers. A little color has returned to his cheeks.

I think he's about to say something, but before he has the chance, the Great Wheel slows to a stop. The same girl who let us on the ride unlocks the door. As soon as she slides it open, the man jumps out and knocks her over. There are shouts of indignation from the crowd as he takes off running, but he's too quick for anyone to stop him.

Every part of me is shaking as I climb out of the gondola. Spencer helps the girl up, then we walk in tense silence down the pier until my legs finally feel like they're going to give out and I have to lean against the wooden railing.

"You're a demon hunter," Spencer says flatly.

Demon hunter?

"We generally go by *exorcist*, but yes," I say, putting a hand to my chest to try to slow my breathing. I'm not sure if my nerves are from another failed exorcism or because Spencer finally knows my secret. "Although, to be honest, I don't go hunting for them so much as they seem to fall right into my lap."

"Were you ever going to tell me?" he asks. His voice sounds guarded. Unfriendly. My heart twists. I knew that expecting him to understand what I do was a long shot, but still, I'm flooded with disappointment.

I swallow. "I was planning to," I say. "I just . . . wasn't sure how."

He doesn't ask me why I do it or who taught me. He doesn't ask me if I'm okay or if I was scared back there. He just shakes his head, like he's trying to clear it. "I, uh. I just need a minute to think," he says.

Tears prick my eyes. His reaction is so much worse than I imagined it would be. I feel like all my organs are being squeezed. He is breaking my heart, and I'm just standing here, letting him do it.

So I turn and walk away. Spencer doesn't try to stop me.

I keep going, but I don't let myself cry until I'm alone in my room, safely buried under the covers. I keep hoping that he'll text me, tell me that he overreacted, that it's no big deal. But he doesn't. Because being an exorcist is a big deal.

A big, relationship-ending deal.

Chapter

17

UNCLE ROY doesn't look up as I slink into the rectory. He's bent over the leather-bound journal I gave him for Christmas last year, scribbling furiously with his fountain pen. I avoided him at church this morning—I knew he'd be mad that I skipped our training session—but I can't avoid him forever.

"Hi," I murmur. I'm still processing what happened with Spencer last night. I'd like to discuss it with Uncle Roy, but he doesn't respond to my greeting and continues to write in his journal.

Yup, he's mad.

Good thing I brought a peace offering. I set a bowl of black jellybeans in front of him. I had to pick through all the other jellybeans to get the black ones so he'd know I care. But he ignores it.

Crap. If he's turning down sugar, it means he's really angry.

I know he won't be able to keep up the silent treatment for long. I just need to wait him out.

I page through a file, pretending to be interested in it, while he continues to write. Eventually, Uncle Roy clears his throat to indicate that he's finally ready to deal with me. I glance at him and give him a sheepish smile. He sets his fountain pen down and gazes at me over the top of his glasses.

The best strategy is to throw myself on his mercy. And if that doesn't work, I'll remind him that the topic of his sermon this morning was forgiveness and that this, right here, is the perfect opportunity to practice what he preaches. So to speak.

"I'm sorry that I missed training yesterday," I say. "But you'll be pleased to hear that I finally finished that report you've been harassing me about—the one on the role of the layman exorcist in the fifteenth century."

I pull the paper out of my bag with a flourish, stand up, and walk it over to him. As if I don't get enough homework at school, Uncle Roy makes me write weekly seven-hundred-fifty-word reports on exorcism-related topics. Lucky for me, his aversion to computers means that he has not yet discovered Wikipedia.

He heaves a heavy, world-weary sigh. "Did you somehow forget that you had a commitment?" He doesn't even try to hide the disappointment in his voice.

I frown. Seriously? I miss one day out of five whole months of training—hardly complaining about all the hours, all the stupid essays, about how practically every second of my spare time has been devoted to training with him—and he's disappointed in me?

"I just needed a day off," I say. "One day. And when I tell you where I was, you'll—"

He holds up a hand to stop me. Then Uncle Roy slides off his glasses and begins to calmly polish them with the soft blue cloth he keeps in his pocket. "I've been thinking. Perhaps it's best if we stop the lessons."

"You mean take a break?" I say. I could get on board with taking a break. Maybe we can skip the training and get serious about finding my mom.

He shakes his head. "No. I mean stop them altogether."

My heart drops. In a million years, this is not what I

expected him to say. "Look, I'm sorry I skipped out on you, but there's no reason we have to quit—"

"Shelby." Uncle Roy gives me a tired smile, and he suddenly looks every one of his seventy-three years. "It's time that we are honest with each other. It seems I've pushed you into this. It's not fair of me to expect you to continue to work at something that you're just not that interested in."

"But—"

"No, it's my fault," he says gently. "I was so sure that this was your path, but I've come to realize that I was wrong. I may have had the best intentions, but I never should have insisted that you commit your future to something just because I felt you should do it. It wasn't my place. I'm sorry for wasting your time."

His words sting. I mean, yeah, he has pushed me, and it's true, I'm not sure that this is what I want to do for the rest of my life, but I am getting better at it. I know I am. And I like that he believes I could be great at it.

I don't want him to stop believing in me.

Unless . . .

I narrow my eyes. "Wait. Is this, like, some kind of reverse psychology or something? You think that telling me I can't train with you anymore will make me want to do it, right?"

Because it's kind of working.

"No," he says, putting his glasses back on and picking up his pen. "I meant every word. We're done. You're free."

I don't feel free. I feel mad. Mad that I've wasted five months, mad that he's giving up on me, all because I missed one lousy session. Mad that I suck so hard at being an exorcist that he no longer wants to train me.

"And now, if you'll excuse me, I have to get back to work." Uncle Roy turns his attention back to his journal, dismissing me.

"Fine," I say. "Wouldn't want to keep you from *your* work." I bend down and pick up Moo from her hiding spot under the desk. It's a small consolation when Uncle Roy starts to sneeze. He's still sneezing when I leave the office, slamming the door behind me.

Chapter

18

I HAVEN'T seen or heard from Spencer since last weekend, when he found out that I'm an exorcist. Yet I still went to the library yesterday for our study session, stupidly hoping he'd be there. But he didn't show up, and obviously the only possible explanation is that he's completely weirded out and no longer wants anything to do with me.

Since it appears that I no longer have study sessions—or training, which I totally regret skipping, because it was so not worth it—I suddenly have a lot of free time on my hands. I've spent every afternoon after school this week wandering around Seattle, partly to avoid going home, where things with Uncle Roy are superawkward, but also because I've been looking for my mom. I've restarted the search for her in all our favorite places. I feel guilty that I've let myself be distracted, that I haven't been out pounding the pavement searching for her every day.

I go into a coffee shop we used to come to, but of course she's not there. I mean, what did I expect? That the demon living inside her would be craving a hazelnut latte?

Even if my mom were here, I don't know what I would do. It's more than likely I would mess up her exorcism, the same way I messed up with Ms. C and the stranger on the Great Wheel.

The coffee shop is crowded. I don't really want a drink, but I stand in line anyway, because being here makes me feel closer to my mom. It also makes me feel desperately lonely. I have never missed her more than I do right this second, which is saying a lot.

I swallow. My throat starts to ache, and I really hope I don't embarrass myself by bawling in front of the barista. I'm debating whether to leave the line and just go home when I finally get a text from Spencer.

My heart leaps. Now that he's had time to process, maybe

he's realized that me being an exorcist is not such a big deal after all.

He wants me to come to a rooftop garden downtown. I shoot him a quick reply to let him know I'll meet him. I'm not too far away, and it only takes me ten minutes to get to the building because I speed-walk the entire way.

It's weird that he wants to meet in this particular building, because it's one I've been in a million times before. My mom worked as a legal secretary in a practice just down the street—being an exorcist doesn't exactly pay the bills, so she had to hold down another job—and I used to meet her in the garden for lunch during the summers sometimes.

I cross the marble lobby and take the elevator all the way up to the twenty-seventh floor. I spot Spencer as soon as the elevator doors slide open, and my heart doubles in speed. He's standing at the railing, staring out toward the thin slice of Elliott Bay that's visible through the surrounding buildings. He turns around when he hears me approach and gives me a small smile.

"Hey," he says.

"Hey." I fiddle with the zipper on my jacket. I glance around the garden—it's been awhile since I've been up here, but it hasn't changed. It's a Garden of Eden in the middle of the city, all perfectly tended grass and trees, polished marble benches. Bright yellow and red tulips grow in big wooden tubs. We're up so high, it feels like we're above the clouds. It smells just like I remember it, too, like flowers and wind.

This afternoon, it's just windy enough to keep the office workers inside. We're alone, aside from a blond guy in aviator sunglasses sitting on one of the benches. Watching us.

Okay, that's creepy.

Why is he staring at us?

Wait. I think it's the guy from the party. The one who interrupted Spencer and me in the cabin. Lucas.

My stomach plummets. If Spencer brought his friend with him, this is not a date. I've totally misread this situation.

Lucas notices me noticing him. He gets up and saunters over to us, and the expression on his face is so serious that my hands start so shake.

What is going on?

"I thought you were going to give us a minute," Spencer says to him, his voice hard.

"You've had plenty of time." Lucas's eyes are hidden behind mirrored lenses. He doesn't crack a smile. "We need to get on with it."

"Get on with what?" I ask, looking back and forth between them. It's pretty clear from the cloud of tension hovering over them that they're not on good terms. "Spencer. What's going on?"

Spencer gazes out at the bay again, like he's gathering his

thoughts. Whatever he's about to tell me is clearly not going to be something I want to hear.

"Just . . . let me explain before you react, okay?" he says, turning back to me.

He pushes up the sleeve of his windbreaker and unclips his antique silver watch, the one he always wears with the face turned to the inside of his wrist. He takes the watch off and shows me a Celtic knot tattoo hidden underneath.

"Okay, so you have a tattoo." Big deal. His brother owns a tattoo shop, so it's not exactly shocking. I reach out to run my finger over his wrist, but he pulls his hand away.

"That's the thing. It's not just a tattoo," he says. "The important part is what it stands for: It's a symbol of protection. Like the rune I made for you."

My fingers fly to the polished stone hanging around my neck. He did mention that the rune was protection from evil spirits.

Lucas sighs. "What Spencer is trying to tell you, in his own convoluted way, is that we're demon hunters." He rolls up his sleeve and shows me the same Celtic knot tattooed on his forearm, only his is a lot larger.

I jerk back, like he's slapped me. Demon hunter is just another name for exorcist.

Spencer's an exorcist.

He shoots Lucas a dirty look. "I was getting to that."

"Were you, though?" Lucas replies. "Cause it kinda seemed like you might chicken out. Again."

A muscle in Spencer's jaw ticks. "I told you, I've been waiting for the right moment."

"You've had two months of right moments," Lucas says.

They're so involved with their bickering that they've forgotten all about me. Which is fine, because it gives me a moment to catch my breath and try to digest this news they've just dropped on me. My legs are shaking, so I walk over to a marble bench and sit down.

Spencer comes over and sits beside me. His knee starts to bounce up and down. "I wanted to tell you," he says.

"Then why didn't you?" He had the perfect opportunity on our date on Saturday, when he found out that I'm in the same line of work. He didn't even try to stop me when I walked away. And then he didn't contact me for days. Spencer knew how upset I was. He knew, but he didn't tell me the truth. Just like Uncle Roy.

I move away from him.

"You took me by surprise," he says. "I mean, I know your Uncle Roy's an exorcist, and I know how your mom felt about keeping you away from the business—"

"Wait," I interrupt, my entire body tensing. "You know my mom?"

"I've met her a few times." Spencer starts to flush.

I stare at him, trying to make sense of the words that have just come out of his mouth. Spencer Callaghan has met my mom more than once. And yet he's never mentioned this to me. Why?

"How much do you know about your mom's . . . situation?" he asks.

"I know everything."

"Then you know she's not in Italy."

"I know *everything*," I repeat. "Now, why did you ask me to meet you here?"

"Because we need your help," Lucas says, walking over to us. "I'm assuming Father Roy must have filled you in on what's happened to Robin."

I keep my expression purposefully blank. I don't trust either of them, and I don't want to volunteer any information about my mom until I know exactly how they want me to help them.

"Father Roy has been training her," Spencer says to Lucas.

I inhale sharply. How does he know that?

Lucas stares at Spencer, dumbstruck. "And you didn't think this was worth mentioning?" he asks. "This is literally the only bit of information you've gathered over the past two months that might have been any help to us."

And there it is. The reason Spencer volunteered to tutor me, all those months ago. It wasn't because he liked me, it was because he wanted to gather information about my mom.

I feel a layer of ice building up around my heart. Spencer doesn't actually have feelings for me. He never cared about me—he's been using me.

Spencer glares at Lucas. "Why do you have to be such a dick?"

"Because, Spencer, finding Robin is critical. It's been our number-one priority for the past five months," he says. "If you'd told Shelby ages ago, like I suggested, maybe we could have—"

"Luke. Shut up." Spencer stands up, his hands balled into fists. He looks as if he'd like nothing more than to knock him out. I've never seen him so riled up, but then again, I guess I don't really know Spencer. I only know the guy he was pretending to be.

I wrap my arms around myself. I'm pretty sure I'm going to throw up.

Spencer notices me shrinking away from him and gains control of himself. "Shelby, it's not what it sounds like," he says. "I mean—okay, at first that's why I . . . but—"

"Just tell me how I can help," I say to Lucas. I can't even look at Spencer. I've been wasting my time on him when I should have been focusing all my attention on getting my mom back.

"Your mom's been spotted in the area," Lucas says. "We thought that if we brought you here, she might show up."

"*You* thought," Spencer says.

They're using me as bait. This is the exact plan I've been pitching to Uncle Roy.

"Do you think she'll show?" I ask.

Lucas holds up his phone. "I'm not picking up any demonic activity," he says. "But it doesn't mean the plan won't work. We'll try again somewhere else, assuming you're up for it."

"Your phone can tell you if there's a demon nearby?"

"We use a demon-tracking app. Lucas developed it." Spencer's voice has a note of grudging respect.

"Yes, I'm amazing. A man of many talents," Lucas says, tucking his phone into his pocket. "Why don't you come back to the cabin with us. We can figure out a plan. We need to fill Mark in on this new development, anyway."

"Mark is an exorcist, too?"

"He's the head of our chapter," Spencer says.

"There are hundreds of us, all over the world. And we're just as good—if not better—than the majority of priests." Lucas smiles. "Speaking of which, maybe you can convince

Father Roy to join us at the cabin. He hasn't been particularly cooperative, but he might listen to you," he says. "You think he'd be more appreciative, considering we're trying to fix his mistake."

Clearly they know that my mom is the portal. And Uncle Roy obviously knows about this demon-hunting group, and yet he's never mentioned them. Irritation surges through me. Another thing he's kept secret from me.

"I can't convince him of anything," I say. "He doesn't even want me involved. I've been searching for my mom on my own."

"That's not a good idea," Spencer says, alarmed.

God, he sounds exactly like Uncle Roy.

I bristle. "Why? You have no idea what I can do."

"No, but we've seen what Robin can do," Lucas says. "We've spent the past few months working to undo the damage she's inflicted. This is a huge mess, Shelby. If we don't find her soon, the entire city is going to be overrun. As I'm sure you know, all she has to do is touch someone for longer than a minute or two and then they're possessed. There's no way you can handle a demon like that on your own."

I scowl at him. This is worse than being lectured by Uncle Roy—and I didn't think anything was worse than that.

The door opens, and a group of people come into the

garden. Spencer takes it as our cue to leave and stands up. "Will you come with us to the cabin?" he asks. "Please."

"Fine." I act like I'm doing them a favor, but really, if I want to find my mom, then this is probably the best way to do it.

This is so not how I expected this afternoon to go.

Chapter

19

"HOW DO you know my mom's still in the city?" I ask, shoving aside Spencer's lacrosse bag and climbing into the back seat of his car. No way am I sitting in the front with Spencer. I don't want to be that close to him right now. "Have you seen her?"

Lucas slides into the passenger seat. "Mark swears he spotted her last week, but she took off before he could get close enough to confirm," he says. "And judging from the sheer amount of demons we've had to expel this week alone, I'd say it's a safe bet that she's still around."

My stomach tightens. "Where did he see her?"

"Now *that* I can't tell you," Lucas says, rolling the window down as Spencer pulls into the street. I'm hit with a blast of cold air that whips my hair around. "It's classified information."

I'm sorry, what?

"Classified from who?" I say, burrowing into my jacket. "She's my mom! I think I'm entitled to know where she is."

"Normally, I would agree with you," he says. "But the fact that you're in the biz . . . well, it casts a different light on this whole situation. We can't have you going off all half-cocked, looking for her on your own."

"I'm not going to go off all half-cocked." Whatever that means.

"To be fair, you did say that you've been looking for your mom on your own," Spencer says, glancing at me worriedly in the rearview mirror. "Which, I have to tell you again, is a *really* bad idea. You have no idea what she's capable of, Shelby. It's much better for everyone if we stick together."

I glare at him. While he's probably right—trying to handle my mom on my own would be insane—I am so sick of everyone acting like they know everything about how to exorcise a demon and that I know nothing. He's only ever seen me at work once, when I tried to deal with the guy on the Great Wheel, but that doesn't count because Spencer was practically catatonic. For all he knows, I could be a master. The greatest exorcist of all time.

And, okay, I've never *successfully* conducted an exorcism on my own. But he doesn't know that. It's so infuriating that he just assumes I can't do it.

"Can you please close the window?" I snap at Lucas. "I'm getting blown away back here."

"Sorry," he says, rolling the window back up. He turns around to face me. "We all have the same goal, Shelby. Working together really is our best chance of getting your mom back."

I know it is, and it's the only reason I agreed to go to the cabin with them. As for us all having "the same goal"—Lucas just reinforced the humiliating reality that Spencer used me to gather information about my mom. I slouch lower in my seat. Once he's helped me get my mom back, I won't have anything to do with him ever again.

Spencer turns a corner a little too sharply. His lacrosse bag slides into me, and something sharp pokes me in the thigh. I unzip the bag and pull out a thick silver crucifix, much bigger and heavier than the one I carry. There's also a set of steel handcuffs and a black leather flask with the initials *M. C.* embossed on it.

Mark Callaghan.

Lucas's revelation that Mark is an exorcist explains a lot about his behavior. Except for one thing. . . .

"Why does Mark have six-six-six tattooed on his wrist?" I ask Lucas.

"That tattoo tricks demons into believing he's one of them," he says. "They see it, they trust him. It's brilliant, actually, because it lets him get close to them. He has them shackled before they even realize what's happening."

"It only works about half the time," Spencer mutters.

"Do you all have one?"

Lucas shakes his head. "No way would I put that sign on my body."

"Mark gets a little carried away with all of this sometimes," Spencer says. I want to ask him what he means by that, but we're already turning down the long driveway that leads to the cabin.

Spencer turns off the ignition. Lucas climbs out of the car and folds the seat forward so I can get out. It smells like pine trees and campfire, that middle-of-the-woods scent that reminds me how secluded this place really is.

I follow them past a row of motorcycles and a huge,

dirty white truck. The cabin looks much shabbier in the daylight. Aside from the freshly painted blue-green door, it's like the place hasn't been touched since it was built in the seventies. The 1870s.

We walk up the wide wooden steps, and Spencer pushes open the door. Just before I walk inside, I notice a row of black iron horseshoes hanging above the entrance. I didn't notice them the last time I was here, maybe because it was dark. Uncle Roy has one hanging above the door of the rectory, just like the ones my mom nailed above all the doors in our house.

My stomach is in knots as I step inside. Unless Spencer or Lucas have covertly texted Mark, he isn't expecting them to bring me here. I'm not sure what his reaction will be when he learns that Uncle Roy has been training me.

The main room is empty, but we can hear voices coming from deep inside the house. Spencer leads us to a large room off the kitchen, where a group of men and women are sitting around a dining-room table. It's the same group I saw the night of the party—two women and the bushy-bearded man who I mistook for a serial killer.

And this is obviously their war room.

There's a whiteboard with a bunch of complicated diagrams on it nailed to one log wall next to a row of muted TV monitors, which are all turned to local news stations. On the other wall, there's a map of Seattle covered in red and green pushpins. Next to the map is a series of small photographs—there must be at least fifty of them. Headshots of people of all ages, including one of my mom.

"Shelby, hey," Mark says. "What a pleasant surprise." His dark hair is hidden beneath a red bandana. He's wearing a long white shirt that covers most of his tattoos, including the mark of the beast on his wrist.

The red-haired woman I recognized from the party—Mark's girlfriend—gives me a wary look. "What is she doing here?"

As if he's wondering that himself, Cerberus starts to growl. He's lying on a fluffy pink dog bed in the corner, a chewed-up plastic bone trapped between his large black paws. Mark turns to scratch him behind the ears, and he quickly settles down.

"Relax, Riley," Lucas says, plunking down into one of the leather desk chairs. He folds his hands on the table. There's a giant symbol carved into the middle of the wood: the same two interlocking circles that are etched on the polished onyx rune that Spencer gave me. "She's one of us."

"And by one of us, you mean what, exactly?" Riley says, narrowing her eyes. In front of her is a stack of yellow file folders. I can tell that they're case files, and the sheer number of them makes me feel faint. They must be working night and day.

Is my mom responsible for all of this?

"Shelby here's a demon hunter," Lucas says, a smile stealing across his face. He's clearly relishing dropping this bit of news on the group.

Spencer gives my arm a quick squeeze as they all turn to stare at me. Heat rises in my cheeks. No one says anything for a minute, and it's superuncomfortable. Then Mark finally breaks the silence.

"Well, I didn't see that coming," he says. "I'm guessing Father Roy's been training you?"

I nod.

"Does he know you're here?" Mark asks.

"Not exactly." I feel a twinge of unease. If Uncle Roy knew I was hanging out with a bunch of laymen demon hunters, I'm pretty sure he'd be so mad that his head would pop off.

"I suppose you brought her here because you think she can help," Riley says to Spencer. Her voice is hostile. I have no idea what she's got against me, but there's definitely something about me that bothers her.

"Obviously," Lucas says. "Shelby is the break we've been waiting for. She's the key to finding Robin. I know it."

"What about all our other cases?" Riley's mouth tightens, and she taps the stack of files with one short green fingernail.

"Riles." Mark reaches across the table and lays his hand over hers. "I promise you, we're not going to forget about Josh."

Beside me, Spencer stiffens. He hasn't said a word since we came in, but I've been aware of him, standing close to me. I hate that I'm aware of him.

"We'll find him," Mark says. "But you know that locating Robin is the priority."

Riley grimaces. I gather that she feels like I'm pushing to the front of the line. It's pretty clear that someone she cares about—this Josh guy, whoever he is—is also possessed. I start to soften toward her. I know what it's like to be in that situation, the dark hole of panic that is so difficult to climb out of. I would do anything to get my mom back, and I can only imagine that she feels the same way about Josh.

"I guess we should introduce you to the team," Mark says to me. "You've met Riley." He rubs her back, and she nods begrudgingly. "And this is Nora and Klaus."

"Hi, Shelby." Nora is around my mom's age. Her hair is cut into a short brown bob, and she's wearing horn-rimmed glasses and a nubby, green cardigan sweater. Klaus is in the same skull-printed suspenders he had on the night of the party, but this time they're holding up a pair of light-blue jeans.

He stands up and offers me his large hand to shake. "Lovely to meet you," he says, smiling widely. He has a gap in between his front teeth. "Anyone hungry? I made some lemon-blueberry muffins earlier."

Everyone seems to get really excited by this. Klaus's muffins are apparently legendary, and judging from the way Nora bounces up and down in her chair, lemon-blueberry is a fan favorite.

While Klaus wanders off to the kitchen, Lucas reaches across the table for a file. He flips it open and groans. "Oh, come on," he says. He holds up the folder; a photo of a guy with long blond hair and a wispy mustache is clipped to the inside cover. "I've fixed this dude three times already. Someone else can take him." He closes the file and tosses it back onto the stack.

"Spencer can handle it," Mark says. He picks up the file and walks over to us. He tries to hand it to Spencer, but he won't take it. He just shakes his head.

"You have to get back to it sometime, brother."

"No, I really don't." From the wary expression that settles over Spencer's face, I don't think this is the first time they've had this argument. His gaze flicks to Riley, but she's staring at the pile of file folders in front of her. It's pretty obvious from the rising flush in her cheeks that she knows he's looking at her. From the way she's avoiding his eyes, I gather that Spencer must be connected to what happened to Josh.

"We need your help," Mark says.

"He *is* helping." Nora shoots Spencer a sympathetic glance. "His protective charms have saved every one of us at one time or another."

Mark sighs. "Okay, yes. The charms are great," he says. "But, Spence, it was one bad exorcism. It's a setback, sure. But it doesn't mean you should quit."

Spencer crosses his arms. "Can we not talk about this right now?"

"I'll do it," I say.

"I don't think that's such a good idea," he says.

"Why not?" I say. "I'm fully capable of conducting an exorcism."

His mouth tightens.

"Don't take it personally, Shelby," Mark says. "He's just worried about you. He's letting his own bad experience—"

"I don't need you to speak for me," Spencer interrupts.

"—get the best of him," Mark finishes.

"Mark, cut him some slack," Lucas says. "Any one of us would be screwed up by what happened."

If Spencer is surprised that Lucas is coming to his defense, he doesn't show it.

"Give me the case back," Lucas says. "Probably easiest if I do it, anyway. I know where to find the guy."

As Mark hands the file to Lucas, Spencer storms out of the room. Mark turns back to me and says, "The best way for you to help is to give us some more information on your mom."

"Like what?"

"Her favorite places, her close friends, anything that might lead us to her."

My heart sinks. Uncle Roy has tried all of this already, has been trying for the past five months. There aren't many areas of the city that are left unturned. "I have a list of every place we've searched for her," I say. I dig in my bag for the copy of my mom's file and hand it to him.

"This is a good start," Mark says, looking it over. "We can cross-reference with our information." He gestures for me to follow him. We walk over to the map.

"What are all the pins for?" I ask.

"The red ones indicate an area of demonic activity." Mark points at a cluster of red pins concentrated in the Fremont area. "The green ones are areas that we've cleared. For now, anyway."

Belltown, Queen Anne, Capitol Hill. All cleared.

"And the yellow pins are places your mom has been known

to frequent before she was possessed." There are only a handful of yellow pins, and most of them are in Fremont. It's where we used to live, before we moved in with Uncle Roy.

"Lucas says you spotted her."

Mark nods. "Last week."

"How did she look?" I glance at the photo of my mom beside the map. It's a printout of her headshot from the website of the law firm where she worked. Her dark hair is pinned back in a bun.

"She seemed okay." He flips through the papers I gave him.

"Define *okay*."

"She's alive," he says, but it doesn't slip past me that he's not meeting my eyes. "Still in one piece."

I'm not sure he's telling the truth, but I can't bear the thought that she's not all right, so I let myself believe him.

Mark grabs a handful of green pins and starts plugging them into different areas of the map. "You and Father Roy have covered quite a lot of ground. I'm impressed."

He assumes that because Uncle Roy has been training me, that means that I'm also involved in the search for my mom. I don't correct him. If Mark hears that Uncle Roy doesn't want me looking for her, it might make him think twice about letting me help them.

"I'm certain that we would have had Robin back long ago

if he'd just work with us," he says with a sigh. "I'll be honest: Your uncle has been a serious pain in my backside."

That sounds about right.

"Why doesn't he want to work together?" I ask.

"He doesn't agree with my approach, even though he's seen the results I get," he says. "I think part of his issue is that we've adopted protection techniques from different areas of the world." He points up at the ceiling. It's painted the same blue-green shade as the tattoo parlor and Spencer's workshop. "Haint blue. An old Southern superstition. Keeps the evil spirits out." He touches the rune hanging around his neck, the same one I'm wearing. "And this here is a Celtic protection charm. For what it's worth, Spencer doesn't make these for just anyone. You must really mean something to him."

Spencer gave me the rune to make me believe he had feelings for me. So that I'd trust him and open up to him about my mom. That's it.

And since Mark is the one who gave Spencer the orders to get to know me, I should be angry with him, too. But he's also trying to find my mom, and that's far more important than my hurt feelings.

"We're going to get her back, Shelby," Mark says, resting his hand on my shoulder. "I promise."

I nod, relieved that he believes we can still save her.

I'm glad someone still believes it's possible.

Chapter

20

I'VE BECOME very adept at avoiding people lately. I've managed to keep from running into Spencer all morning, and considering St. Joseph's isn't a big school, this isn't exactly easy to pull off. He's texted me a bunch of times in the past few days, but I'm not ready to talk to him, so I convince Vanessa to eat lunch with me in Uncle Roy's car instead of our usual spot on the front steps of the school.

"Who are we hiding from?" Vanessa unwraps her bagel,

and the smell of tuna fish immediately stinks up the car. "Sorry," she says. She knows I hate tuna. It's even worse in an enclosed space.

"Spencer." I roll down my window, then busy myself with picking the wilted lettuce off the cheese sandwich I grabbed at the deli across the street.

"What? What happened?"

I take a bite of my sandwich to give myself a second to think. I haven't filled her in on what happened during my date with Spencer yet, mostly because I have no idea what to say to her. The truth is not an option, obviously, but Vanessa can sniff out a lie like a bloodhound. Whatever I tell her, she's probably not going to buy it.

"I just don't think it's going to happen for us," I say. It shouldn't hurt this much, considering Spencer and I were never really together. But my heart doesn't seem to know the difference. And I feel really stupid for believing that his feelings for me were real.

"But why?" Vanessa props her feet up on the dashboard. She's used black marker to shade in the scuff marks on her loafers. Her parents would buy her new ones, but she hates these clunky shoes even more when they're brand-new and have to be broken in. "What aren't you telling me?"

I go to take another bite of my sandwich and give myself

time to compose an answer, but she intercepts my hand before I can get the sandwich to my mouth.

"Sometimes things just don't work out," I say. "It's fine."

Her eyes widen. "Is it Bex Wagner? Did she get to him?"

"No."

"Is Spencer still going to tutor you?"

I hadn't thought about that. I'm probably never going to pass geometry now. "I'll find another tutor."

"I feel like you're not telling me the whole story," she says. Her foot shifts, and I catch a flash of silver writing on the bottom of her loafer.

"What's that on your shoe?" I ask.

"Nothing." Vanessa tries to move her foot to the floor, but I'm too quick for her—I grab her loafer and pull it off.

"Ow, Jesus," she says. "Break my ankle, why don't you?"

I turn her shoe over. On the sole, written in block letters, is the line: *Under love's heavy burden do I sink.*

"Shakespeare?"

"*Romeo and Juliet.*" She snatches her shoe back and slides it on. "Grayson wrote it. It's totally corny, I know. He's totally corny. And ridiculously immature. I don't know what I'm thinking."

"Vanessa, it's okay that you like him. It's more than okay,"

I say, leaning down to stuff my half-eaten sandwich into my bag. "I think it's great."

And I do think it's great. Just because my love life is in the crapper doesn't mean that I want hers to be.

When she doesn't respond, I turn to look at her. My stomach drops. Her face is pale, wiped of expression. She's like a wax figure, an empty shell.

"Vanessa?" I wave my hand in front of her face, but she doesn't even blink. "Vanessa!" I shake her arm, and she startles.

"Huh?"

"Are you all right?"

"Sorry," she says. She rubs her eyes. "Must have spaced out for a second."

"Yeah, you did."

"So Grayson really wants me to go to this basketball game on Friday night," she says. "You and Spencer have to come with us. How'd your date go, by the way?"

Um, what? She doesn't remember that I *just* told her that Spencer and I aren't together?

Okay, don't panic. Just because she checked out for a minute doesn't mean that she's possessed. I haven't noticed any other signs—she doesn't smell, she doesn't have red eyes, her voice sounds normal. She's not ticking any of the boxes.

"Are you sure you're okay?" I ask.

"I'm fine." Vanessa glances down at her half-eaten bagel,

and her brow furrows in confusion. "Oh my God, I'm going to kill Izzy," she says, her eyes narrowing. "She's not going to think eating half of my sandwich is such a funny joke when I get home."

I frown. She doesn't remember eating the first half of her sandwich?

Maybe I should give her a good squirt of holy water, just to be on the safe side. But the bell rings as I'm reaching into my bag for my spray bottle. By the time I've pulled it out, she's already out of the car.

"Crap. I can't be late for my history test," she says.

I relax a little. She remembers that she has a history test. That's good. *She's fine. Clearly I just have demons on the brain.*

Since I have a free period, I'm in no rush to get back into the school, where I might run into Spencer. I hang out in my car, playing the mobile version of *Demon Souls*, the super-addictive demon war game I played at Shane's house, until my next class is about to start.

I lock the car and walk toward the school. I'm the only one in the parking lot besides a woman wearing a ratty old trench coat and a plastic bag on her head who's lurking near the recycling bin. At first, I think she's waiting for me to leave so she can dig through the bin for bottles to return, but just as I'm passing by her, she glances at me, and the world tilts.

It's my mom.

Standing right in front of me.

Wearing a plastic bag on her head.

I'm so stunned, I just stare at her. My chest tightens. And then I burst into tears, because Mark was totally lying. She is definitely not okay. Besides the makeshift rain bonnet, her clothes are supergrungy, and I can tell from her sunken cheeks that she hasn't been eating enough.

This is so much worse than I imagined.

I don't think about the danger or about all the warnings Uncle Roy has given me against approaching demons. Or about how my mom is a portal and if I touch her, I could end up possessed. All I see is my mom. I take a step toward her. I want to hug her, to let her know that it's going to be all right. That we're going to fix her. The fact that she's here, that she found me, must mean that she's still inside there somewhere. I know that she remembers me.

But then our eyes meet, and I stop in my tracks. For a second, my mom's face remains blank. And then she smiles, a smile so terrible, so full of evil, that it makes my blood freeze. Her hands fly up and start to claw at her cheeks. She shakes her head back and forth like a dog, like she's trying to shake off the demon inside of her.

As suddenly as she started, she stops shaking and goes completely still. She looks at me, her expression filled with enough sadness to break my heart. "Shelby." Her voice is pure anguish, but it's my mom's voice, not the voice of a demon, and I can't help it—I take another step toward her. Her eyes darken, and I know I'm losing her again. "Don't follow me," she says, starting to growl. I'm full on ugly-crying as she turns and runs away from me, taking off toward the trail that runs behind the school.

Calm down. Breaking down isn't going to help her. I take a deep, shuddering breath. I should call someone. Uncle Roy. Or Mark. I shouldn't attempt to exorcise her on my own. It's dangerous. I know this, but I reach into my bag for my crucifix anyway.

Neither of them believes I can do it, but neither of them is here. I am. I can't let her get away.

But as I start to run after her, I spot someone walking out of the trees.

My fingers tighten on the crucifix. It's Shane. He's wearing headphones and his head is down, so he doesn't notice my mom charging toward him until she's almost right in front of him.

"Shane, get out of the way!" I yell as I sprint toward them, but he's frozen to the spot, his eyes wide with terror. My mom knocks him over like a bowling pin. There's a spark of red light as her shoulder connects with his. Shane falls to the ground and curls into the fetal position, his hands over his head, as my mom disappears into the trees.

I want to follow her, but I'm not sure I should leave Shane like this. That spark of red light can only mean one thing.

I chew my bottom lip. I'm so close to getting my mom back, but Shane is lying on the ground, totally dazed, and *argh*, I can't just leave him. My mom would want me to help him. And so as she disappears into the trees, I drop my bag and crouch down in front of him, careful not to get too close.

"Are you okay?" I ask.

"I feel kind of funny," he says. His face is pale and his blue eyes are starting to darken, the whites disappearing as his pupils expand.

Awesome. Uncle Roy claimed that my mom had to touch someone for a few minutes in order for a demon to pass through her. But this portal is obviously even more powerful than he suspected.

"Hold still for a minute." I press my crucifix against Shane's bare arm and feel the metal heat up. His skin doesn't burn, though, so I guess the demon hasn't been in him long enough to really make itself at home.

I say the incantation, and Shane's eyes quickly return to their normal color. He tries to sit up, but he's kind of out of it, so I gently push him back down. I'm about to reach into my bag for my holy water so I can finish this off when a hand shoots forward from behind me, holding out the spray bottle.

Chapter

21

I WHIP AROUND. Spencer is standing behind me. He gives me a small smile, but I don't smile back, although it takes everything in me not to. My heart doesn't seem to realize I'm still mad at him.

"What are you doing here?" I ask, snatching my spray bottle from him.

Spencer turns his phone so I can see the map on his screen, zoomed in on the grounds at St. Joseph's. A small cartoon devil hovers over the parking lot. "Remember that demon-detecting app Lucas created?" he asks. "I got a notification right as class started that there was a presence somewhere nearby. When I didn't see you in geography, I figured it was worth investigating. I wanted to make sure you were okay."

My anger at him loosens a little. It's sweet that he wanted to see if I was all right, but one nice gesture doesn't make up for the fact that he knew what was going on with my mom for months and never told me.

"How long have you been standing there?" I ask him as I squirt Shane on the leg with the holy water. No steam rises off his skin, so it seems that I've finally managed to exorcise a demon. Of course, Shane was barely possessed and didn't put up any kind of fight, so I'm not even sure this counts.

"Long enough to see what happened," Spencer replies.

I turn around and glare at him. "Then why didn't you help me?" If he'd stepped in, maybe we could have prevented my mom from running off.

"Because I'm not an exorcist, Shelby," Spencer says. "I can't do it. I'm *never* going to do it again." He shakes his head. "Trust me, I would have only made it worse."

"It can't be any worse," I say. My mom is gone, and who knows if we'll ever find her again. Maybe this was my one chance.

"That's not true," he says. "When I saw what was going on, I called Mark. He's on his way here right now."

Shane slowly sits up. "Hold up," he says, staring at me. His dark hair is flattened on one side, and he has a blade of grass stuck to his face. "You're an exorcist?"

I nod.

"And my mom made you come over that day because she thought I was possessed?"

"Yeah."

He snorts. "Typical." Shane tries to stand, but his legs are wobbly and he falls and lands hard on his butt. "Ow, shit," he says.

Spencer leans down to help him to his feet. "We should probably take you home."

"You take him." I stuff my crucifix and spray bottle back into my bag. "I'm going to wait here for Mark."

Spencer sighs. "Shelby, please just let him handle this," he says. "Mark mentioned that he was going to swing by and pick up Father Roy. The two of them will have it covered. Let them take care of your mom."

"In other words, I should stay out of their way," I say.

"It's probably for the best."

I know he's right—my mom couldn't be in better hands—but still, the thought of just sitting around while they look for her kills me.

"Fine," I say begrudgingly.

"Wait, that lady was your mom?" Shane asks, his eyes widening.

"Yeah."

The horrified expression on his face actually makes me laugh. I get to my feet, and we walk across the parking lot. It's a miracle that no one has seen us, and we're able to get into Uncle Roy's car and away from the school without interference.

"Blech, what's that smell?" Shane asks, rolling down his window.

"Oh. It's tuna," I say. "Blame Vanessa."

It's only a short drive to Shane's house. I wait in the car while Spencer guides Shane inside, concentrating on slowing my breathing. Spencer slowly walks back toward the car, his hands stuffed in his pockets, and I'm pretty sure we're about to have "a conversation."

And sure enough, as soon as he climbs into the passenger seat, he says, "I know I haven't handled any of this very well." He rubs the back of his neck. "Believe it or not, I was planning to tell you everything."

I back out of Shane's driveway. "Seems like being trapped on a Ferris wheel with a demon might have been the perfect opportunity." *Instead of letting me feel like a freak.*

He blows out a long breath of air. "In retrospect, yes. But, in my defense, I wasn't thinking straight. If you recall, I was barely holding it together that night." His face flushes. "When I realized you were an exorcist, I panicked. I felt like an idiot because I'd spent two months getting to know you and I never picked up on it," he says. "And I knew that if I told you about my family, you'd automatically assume that I was only hanging out with you to get information on your mom—"

"Which you were."

He grimaces. "Yes, but that wasn't . . ." He glances out the window before looking back at me. "For what it's worth, I'm sorry."

My heart starts to pound painfully. He kept the fact that he knew my mom was possessed from me for months. He wants to be my friend? He needs to trust me enough to tell me what happened to make him turn away from exorcism.

"Who's Josh?" I ask.

When Spencer doesn't immediately respond, I think he's going to shut down, shut me out again, but he surprises me. "Riley's brother," he says. "I never should have tried to handle him on my own. I knew better. Rule number one: Always work in pairs."

"What happened?"

He leans his head against the back of the seat. "Mark had just started dating Riley. I didn't know Josh well; I'd only met him a couple of times. One night I saw him at a party. He was acting really weird, but I figured he was probably on something. Then I saw his eyes, and . . . well. It was clear that drugs were not the problem," he says. "Instead of calling Mark and waiting for him to get there so we could exorcise him together, I got cocky. I figured I didn't need Mark; I could do it myself."

I think about Ms. C and how I tried to handle her by myself. And how much worse it could have been if I hadn't called Uncle Roy.

"It didn't work. Obviously. Josh crashed through the second-floor window in the bedroom I'd taken him to. He took off, and, long story short, no one has seen him since," he says. "That was more than a year ago."

My stomach tightens. I know exactly how it feels to worry about someone, to not know where they are. It must be even worse for Spencer, who's weighted down by guilt. Just like Uncle Roy.

"It's better for everyone if I stick to protection charms," he says. "At least I know I can do that properly."

We should probably talk about this in more depth, but we're already back at the school. I pull up beside Spencer's car.

"So why do you do it?" he asks me.

"At first, it was only because Uncle Roy believed I

would be good at it," I say, slowly. "But now . . . I don't know. I think maybe I could be good at it." If Uncle Roy would continue to train me, I might even be great at it. "It doesn't matter, though, because, what happened with Shane aside, I don't think I'm going to do it anymore."

"Why not?"

I shrug. Now I'm the one blocking Spencer out. But I don't think I can tell him that Uncle Roy no longer believes in me without crying. He spent a lot of time and effort training me, and he was right: I didn't take it seriously. I blew him off, like it wasn't important—like *he* wasn't important.

I owe him an apology. And if Uncle Roy decides never to train me again, well, I guess I'll have to live with that.

"If you don't want to go to class, I could come home with you," Spencer says. "Keep you company."

I appreciate the offer, but I'm still shaken from seeing my mom and I just want to be alone. Also, my feelings for Spencer are all mixed up and until I work them out, hanging out with him one-on-one is probably not the best idea.

"I'll be fine," I say.

He gives me a sad smile. I watch him climb out of the car, wishing that everything between us weren't so complicated.

At home, I grab a legal pad from the rectory and then head to the screened-in porch. I need to do something to keep busy, so I might as well get a head start on writing the report.

Yes. I am so desperate for something to keep me busy that I'm doing paperwork.

Case Number: *EX104-17-3841*
Incident: *The Exorcism of Robin Black*
Exorcist: *Who knows*

At around 1200 hours on May 29, I was eating lunch in my car (well, in Father Roy's car) in the St. Joseph's school parking lot. (Note to Father Roy: I realize I broke one of your cardinal rules—eating in your precious Honda— but I want to report everything as accurately and honestly as possible, even if that means putting myself in front of the oncoming train of your wrath. Also, if your car still stinks, it's because Vanessa had tuna fish.) I first noticed a woman lurking around the recycling bins when I was walking back into the school. When I got closer, I

*realized it was my mother, Robin Black.
The reason I didn't recognize her at
first was because she was wearing a
plastic bag on her head, which is
something she would **never** do if she
weren't possessed.*

I close my eyes. I want to believe that when Uncle Roy comes home, he'll have my mom with him. But just thinking about how she looked when I saw her and the tight grip that demon had on her makes me feel so hopeless.

I start to bawl. I cry until my eyes ache, and then I fall asleep, my head resting awkwardly against the back of the chair.

And when I wake up, hours later, it's dark outside and someone is banging on the front door.

Chapter

22

I WALK down the hall, still half-asleep. I flick on the porch light, and I see Vanessa through the little rectangular glass panels set into the door. She jiggles the door handle impatiently.

"Just a second," I say. I'm surprised to see her, because she never drops by unannounced. She's too afraid she'll run into Uncle Roy.

As soon as I get the door open, Vanessa lurches toward

me. She's still wearing her school uniform, along with a pair of turquoise aviator sunglasses. Her hair is a tangled mess.

"Let me guess. . . . You were out with Grayson. Were you guys rolling around in a field or something?" I say, picking a leaf out of her bangs.

As a response, Vanessa lets out a monster belch, so big and thunderous that it practically blows my hair back. The smell of beer emanates off her, so strong that I have to hold my nose.

Great, she's drunk. I guess that's why she came here instead of going home.

"All right, so that was seriously gross," I say. "What is up with you lately?"

She doesn't answer; she just gives me a weird, lopsided smile. She pushes past me, kicking off her black loafers, and stumble-walks down the hall toward my room, making retching noises.

"Vanessa, *please please please* don't throw up in my room," I say, darting into the kitchen to grab a blue bucket from under the sink. If Uncle Roy shows up to find her drunk, he will for sure tell her parents and they will kill her and that will be the end of my only friend in the world.

When I get into my room, Vanessa is trying to open the window. It's chilly out, but maybe the cold air will settle her stomach. She seems to be having trouble getting the window open, so I set the bucket on my desk and walk over to help her.

She collapses onto my bed. Moo lets out a yowl and darts out from underneath my duvet. I reach down to pick my cat up, but she's frozen, her ears pinned against her head. The hair on her back is raised in a stiff white ridge, and her green eyes are laser-focused on Vanessa. She starts to hiss.

Moo never hisses at anyone—certainly never Vanessa. She loves Vanessa.

A bad feeling settles over me. Animals can sense a supernatural presence—it's one of the first things that Uncle Roy taught me when I started training. I think it's part of the reason why he let me keep Moo, even though he's "allergic."

When I look at Vanessa, she's staring into space with the same blank look on her face that she had during lunch this afternoon. I pick Moo up just as Vanessa leans forward and hisses back at her. My cat squirms in my arms, desperate to get away, and Vanessa laughs this weird, witchy cackle that makes the hair on my neck stand up. It freaks Moo out so bad that she scratches me in her panic to get away. She jumps out of my arms and bolts out the door.

"Ow!" A line of scratches appear on my forearm.

Vanessa is practically asphyxiating with laughter, like my cat scratching the hell out of me is the funniest thing she's ever seen. Then her face instantly straightens, all the emotion wiped away. She's still as a statute.

I don't want to leave her alone, but my arm is bleeding. I grab an old T-shirt and press it against my skin while mentally running through my "so you think you might be dealing with a demon" checklist:

1. Smells like sulfur. I can't smell anything but alcohol. That doesn't mean Vanessa doesn't smell like sulfur—it just means that the alcohol could be masking it.

2. Talking in a strange voice. So far she hasn't said a word—which is very unlike her—so I can't determine if her voice has changed.

3. Demon eyes. This is the most foolproof sign of demonic possession, but I don't know if Vanessa has shark eyes or not because she's wearing sunglasses. And the only way I'm going to know for sure is if I take them off of her.

I swallow and say a quick prayer. Vanessa doesn't object or slap my hand away when I remove her sunglasses, like she might have under normal circumstances. She just lets me slide them off.

And when I see her eyes—her blown-out pupils—I know for certain that this situation is NOT GOOD. Not good at all.

Okay, think.

The first thing I need to do is call Uncle Roy. Uncle Roy will fix this.

I grab my cell phone, but Vanessa suddenly jerks to life, like she's just been rebooted. Her mouth twists into a ghastly smile, and it changes her face so much that she doesn't even look like herself anymore. Her forehead and cheeks start to bubble, like water is boiling under her skin, which is supergross.

So it turns out that waiting for Uncle Roy to get home isn't going to be an option. I'm going to have to do something right now, even though I feel completely out of my element.

"Vanessa, I'm so glad you came by because I need some help with my physics homework." I smile at her—*everything's fine, nothing to worry about*. "Just let me grab my textbook. . . ." My hands are shaking as I dig in my bag. My handcuffs aren't going to be of any use—there's nothing to handcuff her to in my room—so hopefully my cross and a good squirt of holy water will be enough to subdue her until Uncle Roy eventually gets here. My fingers close around the spray bottle just as she ascends to the ceiling, legs crossed.

I hold the bejeweled spray bottle in one hand and my cross in the other. I stand underneath her, just far enough away that she won't be able to grab me. Vanessa flips upside down so she's sitting on the ceiling. Her skirt flips, too, hanging down to her chest, so thank god she's wearing boxer shorts underneath. Her long dark hair sways like seaweed. "You think you can get rid of me so easily?" Her voice is deep, growly—much how I imagine a wolf would sound, if it could speak—and her eyes are now two burning red coals.

I haven't forgotten that everything always goes sideways whenever I try to exorcise someone, and I'm not totally sure I can help Vanessa, but I have to do something.

I hold up my spray bottle. "*Deus, audi oratiónem meam; áuribus pércipe verba oris mei,*" I say. I spray her, but I'm so nervous that my aim is off. Vanessa dodges the water and scuttles across my ceiling like a cockroach.

"*Nam supérbi insurréxerunt contra me, et violénti quæsierunt vitam meam.*" I aim again, and this time a jet of holy water arcs through the air and hits her square on the shoulder. She screams as the water soaks through her T-shirt. She drops to the ground, inches from me, and I don't think I'm overstating anything when I say that she is furious.

I am pee-my-pants terrified, but I hear Uncle Roy's voice

in my head reminding me to stay calm. Don't panic. You can do this.

You can do this.

You have to.

"*Nam supérbi insurréxerunt contra me, et violénti quæsierunt vitam meam,*" I say, but my voice wobbles. Vanessa cocks her head to the side, studying me. And then, quick as lightning, her hand shoots out. But instead of her fingers closing around my throat, her hand slams into an invisible wall. For a moment, we stare at each other, like neither of us can believe what just happened. Then she tries to grab me again.

Same result.

I touch the protection rune Spencer made me.

Huh. I guess it really works. . . .

Vanessa screams in frustration at not being able to choke me to death. Then she starts to twist around the room, destroying everything in her path. In a matter of seconds, she completely trashes my room—ripping the posters off my walls, tearing my duvet so the feathers come out, overturning my wastebasket. For the grand finale, she jumps on top of my desk, then leaps into the air and back down onto the wooden top. It splinters underneath her feet, as easily as if she'd just snapped a branch.

And now I'm angry. I know it's not Vanessa's fault—she is possessed, after all—but that desk was a gift from my mom. She is *so* going to pay for that after she's healed.

"*Ecce, Deus ádjuvat me, óminus susténtat vitam meam,*" I say. The prayer doesn't seem to be slowing her down. She grabs my biology textbook and rips it in two like it's no big deal, then tosses the pages into the air.

I continue to chant, and she continues to ruin everything she comes in contact with. I spray her a few more times with the holy water, but I really don't seem to be getting anywhere, so I'm super-relieved when Uncle Roy finally gets home. He obviously hears the commotion, because he runs into my room. In one glance, he takes in the situation and draws his cross from his pocket.

Now she's going to get it.

"Shelby, stand back," Uncle Roy says, but the words are barely out of his mouth before Vanessa comes at him. She smacks him aside as easily as if she were swatting a fly. Uncle Roy sails through the air, and his head knocks against the wall with a sickening *thud*. He slumps forward, out cold.

Oh. Shit.

I rush over to him. Vanessa doesn't attempt to come at me again; she just tears the curtains hanging from the rod above my door right off and charges down the hall. A few seconds later, I hear glass smashing, something heavy being turned over, and then the back door banging against the wall.

And she's gone.

Chapter

23

UNCLE ROY isn't waking up. I slap his cheeks to try and rouse him. "Wake up wake up wake up wake up! Please wake up!"

Nothing.

I slap a little harder.

Still nothing.

Okay, don't panic. He's breathing—I can see that his chest is rising and falling beneath his sweater—but he's superpale.

I reach for my spray bottle and squirt him square in the

face. He sputters, gradually coming to, but his eyes aren't focusing.

That can't be good.

I reach for what's left of my pillow and put it under his head, then I spread my shredded duvet cover over his legs. I read somewhere that people in shock should be covered with a blanket, although I have no idea why, nor do I have any idea if he is actually in shock.

But I sure am.

Uncle Roy is old, but he's always seemed so strong to me. Invincible. I never expected him to be knocked down in the first round. And by Vanessa, of all people!

I pull out my cell phone and dial 9-1-1. As I'm giving the emergency-response lady our address, Uncle Roy's eyes flutter shut again. I shake him and yell "Don't fall asleep!" in his ear, because what if he has a concussion?

He groans. "I'm not deaf, Shelby." He struggles to sit up, but I gently push him back down. He could have broken something, and I don't want him to do further damage to himself by trying to get up.

"The ambulance is on its way."

"There's really no need. I'm fine," he says, but his arm is bent at a weird angle. He sinks back down with an exasperated sigh, clutching his elbow. "You have to go after Vanessa."

"What's the point? I tried to exorcise her. It didn't work. Again," I say. "Besides, I'm not leaving you here alone."

"Shelby, there's no time to argue. You can do this," he says. "You have to help that poor girl."

"I can't help her! Have you forgotten that I've never been able to help anyone, ever?"

He reaches over and squeezes my hand. "You can do it. I know you can. I *believe* you can."

My eyes unexpectedly sting with tears. I'm not so sure that I can do it despite what he says, but I don't want to disappoint him. I'd like to linger in this Hallmark moment for a while longer, but he flaps his good hand impatiently at me to get going.

"What are you going to tell the paramedics?" My room looks like a hurricane passed through it. How is he going to explain this mess?

"I'll think of something," he says. "Now go on."

I stuff my holy water back into my messenger bag but keep my crucifix out. Wincing, Uncle Roy slides his hand into his pocket and pulls out his worn black Bible.

"For extra protection," he says, gesturing for me to take it. "And, Shelby, don't forget to—"

"Use the handcuffs," I say, sticking the Bible into my bag. "I know." I give him a quick kiss on the cheek and take off after my friend.

✗ ✗

I'm standing on the front porch, surveying our yard. Vanessa is nowhere to be seen. She could be long gone—she's a marathon runner—but as I stare at the cemetery, I get goose bumps. I think she might be in there.

My legs are shaking as I walk across the grass. I pass through the wrought-iron gate, which is floating crookedly on its hinges. I'm not more than a few feet into the graveyard when I notice that a couple of the gravestones have been knocked over. Now, these gravestones are made of marble and weigh approximately a thousand pounds each. You can barely move them with a backhoe, never mind yank them out of the ground yourself. Unless you're a demon with superhuman strength.

I'm on the right track.

My messenger bag bangs against my thighs as I make my way down the twisting path between the graves. I've got a tight hold on my cross because my palms are so sweaty that I'm afraid I'll drop it. Vanessa could be hiding anywhere here—or nowhere here. I'm half-expecting her to jump out from behind a gravestone and half-convinced that she's long gone and I will never see her again.

I hear sirens approaching. Good, the ambulance is close.

I stop in front of a small mausoleum, which was built in

the early nineteenth century. It's been awhile since I've been in the graveyard—I make it a point not to come through here if I can help it, because *graveyard*—but I know that the marble angel guarding the door definitely had wings the last time I saw her. And sure enough, when I glance down, I find what remains of her wings, shattered into a million pieces.

The stone door of the mausoleum is slightly ajar, so all signs point to Vanessa being inside. I have only ever been in there once—with her, years ago. She dared me to go in with her, but we lasted less than ten seconds before the realization dawned that we were basically in a house of the dead. Much screaming ensued, and we swore we would never venture anywhere near this crypt ever again.

But here I am. About to go inside.

Every instinct is telling me to run, far and fast, but I can't turn back. Not when I know Vanessa needs my help.

So I take a deep breath and, heart beating wildly, push open the door.

The room is so dark that it's like walking into a coal mine. I pull my phone out of my pocket and turn on the flashlight app. I hold it up, letting the beam of light crisscross the space until it finds Vanessa. She's standing in the corner with her back to me. Staring at the wall. She doesn't move.

While I'm relieved to have found her, there is something so profoundly eerie and *Blair Witch Project*–esque about her stillness. It freaks me out more than when she was tearing up my room.

Maybe I can whisper the incantation from here. I mean, who's to say I have to speak the words loudly for them to be effective? Maybe whispering works just as well. I could hit her with it before she even knows I'm in the room.

I start to say the incantation under my breath so quietly that the sound doesn't even reach my own ears.

I have witnessed enough exorcisms to know that demons do not go gently into that good night—you have to drag them to it. Vanessa hasn't moved—she's still facing the wall—so I'm pretty sure that means silently chanting isn't going to work. I'm going to have to say it louder, but before I do that, I'm going to need to restrain her.

I walk toward the large, white marble coffin that sits on a dais in the center of the room. I try not to think about what's inside the coffin as I carefully set my bag on top. I shine the light over the marble, and sure enough, there's a brass handle on the side that I can handcuff her to. Iron would be better, but brass can be used to drain some of her superhuman strength in a pinch.

My plan is to sneak up behind her and slap the handcuffs on, blind her with holy water, and then drag her over to the coffin and chain her to it. Once I have her secured, I'll start the incantation.

It should work. I mean, it hasn't ever worked before, but I'm going to try to not let that affect my confidence.

I fish my handcuffs and spray bottle out of my bag, juggling them along with my crucifix and phone as I walk around the side of the coffin. I'm right behind Vanessa when, thanks to my sweaty palms, I lose my grip. My stomach clenches as my phone drops to the cement floor with a clatter. Plunging us into total darkness.

This is not good.

I drop to my knees, scouring the ground. I have to find my phone.

"Shelby?" Vanessa's voice is right near my ear, which makes my heart stop. "What's happening to me?" She sounds small and scared, and for a second I wonder whether the whispered incantation really worked. But then I feel Spencer's rune heating up my neck. The way the stone is warming up right now makes me think that this is a trick—that whoever is speaking to me right now is not Vanessa.

My fingers finally close around my phone. Somehow it's still working. I turn the flashlight back on and shine the beam directly into her glowing red demon eyes. She doesn't even blink.

"You think you're going to squat inside my best friend," I say, snapping one of the handcuffs on Vanessa's wrist.

Not today, Satan. Not today.

She laughs. "You think these stupid little handcuffs are going to hold me?"

"Oh, I know they will," I say, yanking her toward the coffin. "They're made of steel and blessed by a priest. There's no way out." I snap the other end of the handcuffs on to the brass handle of the coffin. "Now, let's send you back to hell where you belong."

Vanessa tugs on her arm so hard, the coffin shifts. Okay, so she still has plenty of superhuman strength. I guess brass isn't as effective as iron.

I'd better do this quickly.

I hold up my crucifix. *"Deus, in nómine tuo salvum me fac, et virtúte tua age causam meam. Deus, audi oratiónem meam; áuribus pércipe verba oris mei."*

Vanessa throws her head back and howls—an ear-splitting, inhuman sound that echoes through the chamber.

"Nam ex omni tribulatióne eripuit me, et inimícos meos confúsos vidit óculos meus!"

She continues to yank on the coffin. I'm worried that she'll pull it right over and whatever—whoever—is inside will be joining our party. But then her body starts to buck and she begins frothing at the mouth like a rabid dog.

Her entire body stiffens, then suddenly relaxes. Vanessa's eyes roll back into her head, and she slumps to the ground, totally limp.

I poke her gently in the leg with the end of my crucifix. She doesn't scream in pain, but just to be sure the demon's really gone, I take the lid off the spray bottle and dump the rest of the holy water on her head, completely drenching her. There's no hissing, no burning. Nothing but rivulets of water running down her face.

I sag down beside her, my legs weak. I have no idea how I'll explain what just happened to her when she comes to or my role in all of this. I just hope she takes the news better than Spencer did.

Chapter

24

I'VE CLEANED up my room as best I can. My sheets and pillow are too far gone to save, and my desk is definitely beyond repair. I had to throw out my biology textbook and a pair of jeans that Vanessa managed to rip right through the crotch. There are claw marks in my mattress, but she didn't flip it over, so my mom's file, which is hidden underneath the bed with *Rituale Romanum*, are both still in one piece.

I haul the garbage bag filled with my ruined stuff into

the kitchen and drop it near the back door. Uncle Roy is standing at the counter, trying to make toast. His right arm is in a sling—Vanessa fractured his elbow and gave him a good-size goose egg on the back of his head. He's like a bird with a broken wing, and watching him struggle to spread butter on his toast is the saddest thing ever. It's so sad, in fact, that I'm not even going to grill him about where the butter came from. I'm just grateful that he wasn't hurt worse; I don't think I could have handled it if he were more seriously injured.

"Let me do that," I say, taking the knife from him and shooing him over to the table. "You know you're not supposed to exert yourself."

The doctor instructed him to rest, but—shocker—Uncle Roy isn't cooperating. He can't seem to sit still. I caught him trying to work on a painting earlier this morning. I think it was a sunflower, but I can't be sure, as it mostly just looked like a big yellow blob.

Uncle Roy winces and clutches his side as he lowers himself into his chair. I scrape off half of the butter he slathered on the toast—seriously, he is just asking for clogged arteries—then set the plate in front of him. I offer to get him a glass of prune juice to wash it down with, but instead of thanking me, he just scowls. You would think he'd be a little bit grateful that I care about the health of his bowels; instead he acts like I'm trying to poison him or something.

I pour myself a bowl of bran cereal, just to set a good example, and sit down across from him.

"Did you finish the report?" he asks as soon as my butt hits the chair.

After we got home from the hospital, we were up for most of the night, going over every detail of what happened with Vanessa. I've barely had any sleep. I spent most of the morning cleaning up my room, and the second I sit down, he asks me if I've written the stupid report?

"I'll get to it," I say. I even smile when I say it, like I can't wait to capture every moment of one of the scariest nights of my life on paper.

"You should write it down while it's still fresh."

I grunt. We eat in silence for a few minutes.

I fiddle with the rune around my neck. There's one part of the story I didn't tell him, but only because I didn't remember it until this very minute. "Something weird happened when Vanessa tried to grab me," I say. "She couldn't reach me—it was like there was a wall between us."

Uncle Roy's eyes flick to the rune. "You got that from the Callaghan boy, I assume," he says. "I've heard that the younger one makes protection charms."

This is the first time he's brought up the Callaghans. I did most of the talking last night, filling him in on Vanessa's exorcism. Uncle Roy did not return the favor by telling me what happened with my mom when he was out with Mark, other than to say that they couldn't find her. I didn't want to push him too hard, because he was obviously in a lot of pain.

"Yes."

He nods begrudgingly. "The workmanship is excellent."

"I can ask Spencer to make you one."

"I don't need a protection charm," he says gruffly. "I'm much too good at what I do."

"Says the guy with the fractured elbow."

He smiles sheepishly. "I admit, I was a bit off my game last night."

A bit? He didn't even have the chance to start the incantation before Vanessa took him out.

"You didn't tell me that the Callaghan boy was tutoring you." Uncle Roy fixes me with his laser stare, and I shift in my seat. "Or that you were working with them," he says.

"I was going to tell you. . . ." Someday.

He sighs. "Well, while I don't approve of Mark's methods, I haven't had much luck exorcising Robin on my own, so I've agreed that it's time we all worked together," he says. "And as it looks like I'll be laid up for a while, I shall act as a consultant on the case. Mark will take over your training. Just until I get back on my feet."

He wants me to train with Mark?

"Wait. I thought you didn't want me training at all anymore," I say.

"Yes, well, after what happened with Vanessa last night, I've changed my mind. As long as you are still interested in learning and you promise not to miss any more sessions, I think you should continue to train," he says. "But, Shelby, let me be very clear: You may train with Mark, but you are not to work on your mother's case."

"Okay," I say. I can't stop from smiling. I'm so relieved that he's forgiven me. And that he believes in me again. All the tension drains out of my body. I get up and go around the table to give him a hug, but it's a weak one because I don't want to hurt his arm. But Uncle Roy pulls me in tighter, like he's afraid to let me go. And for the first time, it hits me that maybe he needs me just as much as I need him.

Chapter

25

MARK DOESN'T waste any time scheduling my first lesson. He calls the next afternoon when I'm in the middle of doing my history homework after school.

"Be ready in five minutes," Mark says. "We're coming to pick you up."

He hangs up before I can ask him who "we" is or where we're going.

I feel a fissure of excitement as I stuff my bejeweled spray bottle and crucifix into my messenger bag. For a minute I wonder if he's bringing Spencer and my heart kicks up, but then I remember what happened with Riley's brother and that Spencer's done with training, so he probably wouldn't be interested in tagging along.

I find Uncle Roy in the living room, reading a paperback in his recliner. He told me earlier that he's decided to "enjoy his convalescence," which for him seems to mean reading John le Carré novels and steadily making his way through the cloth-lined basket of baked goods that Klaus dropped off while I was at school today.

"Mark called," I say, grabbing a giant oatmeal-chocolate-chip cookie from the basket.

He sets his book facedown in his lap. "Yes, he called me, too," he says. "Now, Shelby, remember—"

I roll my eyes. "I know, I know. I'm there to observe, not participate." I take a bite of the cookie and a groan escapes me; it's just that good. Klaus should seriously consider opening a bakery.

Uncle Roy looks like he's about to say something else—probably to tell me for the billionth time not to get my hopes up that we'll find my mom—when he's distracted by thumping music coming from the street. He pulls back one of the filmy white curtains, frowning at the blast of death-metal music emanating from the huge white truck with tinted windows that has just parked in front of our house.

"This is only until I'm back on my feet," he says, letting the curtain drop.

I lean over and give him a kiss on the cheek. "Be home in a few hours."

"Shelby?"

I turn around.

"Be careful."

I nod. I know it must be killing him to have to sit on the sidelines.

The death metal abruptly stops as I walk out of the house. Mark gets out of the passenger side of the truck. He's in jeans and a fisherman's vest, a black beanie pulled low over his forehead. A plain wooden cross sticks out of the side pocket of his vest. The cross looks crudely made, nothing like the ornate silver crucifix I carry.

"Afternoon," Mark says. He's wearing mirrored sunglasses, even though the sky is overcast, and I can see myself reflected in the lenses. I look nervous. Probably because I am nervous.

He folds down the seat so I can climb into the back. Nora gives me a sunny smile from the driver's seat. "Hi, Shelby."

"Hi," I say. And then I spot Spencer sitting in the back

seat. I'm surprised to see him, even though I'd wondered if he'd come.

"Hey," he says.

"What are you doing here?"

"I asked him to join us," Mark says. "It's about time he started training again."

Spencer shakes his head. "I didn't agree to this."

Okay, wait. If he's not going to train, then why is he here?

Before I can ask him, Mark turns around to look at us. "The number-one rule is that we always work in pairs," he says. "Shelby, you're with me today. Spencer, you and Nora need to stick together."

"Mark, I told you, I'm not going to—"

"This is for safety reasons," Mark interrupts. "You just can't predict what a demon will do. It never hurts to have backup."

Spencer gives Mark a dirty look. Maybe he takes this as an admonishment for the time he tried to exorcise Riley's brother on his own. But I think Mark means it as a warning for me—Uncle Roy probably told him that I went rogue and tried to take care of Ms. C by myself.

"Normally I would ease you into things, Shelby—start you off with the history of exorcism and all the theory behind what we do," Mark says. "But I understand that Father Roy has already taught you most of that."

I nod.

"Now, I should explain that I have some unorthodox methods for hunting demons," he says. He whips off his sunglasses. His eyes are completely black, thanks to contact lenses. He gives me a twisted smile that shows all his teeth. Combined with his shark eyes, it's hard to believe that he's not possessed.

I shudder. "That's creepy."

Mark laughs. "But effective," he says. "When I wear these babies, I can get up close and personal with demons."

"Like with your tattoo?"

He holds up his arm to show me the ink on his wrist. "Exactly."

"So where are we going, anyway?" I ask as Nora pulls on to the freeway.

"Fremont," she says, merging into traffic. "It's a hotbed of demonic activity. And we got a tip that your mom's been hanging out there recently."

Spencer reaches over and squeezes my hand, a show of support, and my heart melts a little. I'm still upset with him for not telling me that he's an exorcist, too, and for befriending me just so he could find out information about my mom. But he's making it very hard to hang on to my anger.

"We're hoping that if we get the two of you in the same area, we can draw her out," Mark says.

It's the same plan Lucas had on the rooftop garden. I hope it works this time.

Nora swerves into a parking spot in front of a coffee shop, deftly squeezing the truck into a space between two cars. We get out of the truck, and Mark pulls out his phone. His eyebrows fly up into his hairline. "Well, folks, we've got our work cut out for us today," he says, turning his phone around to show us the screen. Lucas's demon app is showing at least twenty cartoon demons on the map.

"There's one right behind you," Spencer says.

Mark turns. I look over his shoulder at the guy leaning against the brick wall of the coffee shop. He's not much older than I am. He looks like a frat boy, dressed in khaki shorts and a faded gray T-shirt with *I Don't Get Drunk, I Get Awesome* written in red letters across the chest. His hair is tucked under a Seattle Mariners ball cap. Oh, and he has the telltale blank stare of the possessed.

"All right, Shelby," Mark says, gesturing at the guy. "Let's see what you can do."

Um, what?

"You want me to perform this exorcism?"

Mark nods. "Yup."

"But we're in the middle of the street," I say. "Someone's going to see."

"We'll block you." Nora gently nudges me forward. "Just be quick about it."

I take my crucifix out of my bag. I slowly walk forward, and Nora, Spencer, and Mark form a circle behind me. The sidewalk is narrow, and I'm standing uncomfortably close to the guy. My skin prickles.

Okay, I managed to exorcise Vanessa on my own; I should be able to take care of this dude. The difference today is that I have an audience. I'm very aware of Spencer and the others standing behind me. Watching me.

"*Deus, audi oratiónem meam; áuribus pércipe verba oris mei,*" I say.

The demon snaps to attention. Frat boy focuses his black eyes on me, his expression eerily blank as he starts to claw at his face, leaving livid red scratches down his cheeks.

"*Nam supérbi insurréxerunt contra me, et violénti quæsierunt vitam meam.*"

Suddenly, he starts to retch. He hunches over and throws up on the sidewalk, and I jump back to avoid getting vomit on me. Spencer is right behind me, and he puts a steadying hand on my back.

"Keep going," he says. "You've almost got him."

This little bit of encouragement convinces me to continue. I lift the cross a bit higher, preparing to say the incantation again.

"What's going on here?" I hear someone say. I whip around, and there's a policeman standing beside Mark. He grimaces at the sight of the frat boy puking his guts out. Then his gaze flicks to the crucifix in my hands, and his expression hardens.

"Officer," Mark says. "We're trying to help this gentleman." He moves to shield me so that I can finish the exorcism. I quickly say the last few words of the incantation, and frat boy groans and slumps against the brick wall. My holy water is in my bag, but I don't dare reach into it while the policeman is here, so I stretch and touch the arm of my crucifix to the guy's bare leg. When his skin doesn't bubble or burn, I relax.

I smile. Either that demon was particularly easy to expel, or I'm getting better at this. I can't wait to tell Uncle Roy.

I turn to join the others, and that's when I spot my mom, who's watching us from the other side of the street. I gasp. She's no longer wearing a plastic bag on her head, but she still has that ratty old raincoat on. She takes off as soon as she realizes that I've seen her.

Mark and Nora are preoccupied with talking to the policeman. I can't let my mom get away again, so I immediately start running after her.

"Shelby, wait!" Spencer calls.

But I'm already halfway down the street. I can hear Spencer running to catch up with me.

"We have to wait for Mark and Nora," he says.

"We don't have time!" How does he not understand that? My lungs feel like they're about to burst, but I run faster because we have to catch up to her.

We run down Fremont Avenue. When she turns left onto 36th Street, I suddenly know exactly where she's headed.

"She's going to the troll." My mom used to bring me to the Fremont Troll when I was a kid. I loved climbing on the massive stone troll underneath the Aurora Bridge. A bunch of local artists built him in the early nineties.

It's beginning to get dark out, so that works in our favor—it means that there probably won't be many other people down there. I don't want to get stopped again.

"Okay, just let me tell Mark where we're at," Spencer says, panting. He pulls out his phone and shoots Mark a quick text.

We head underneath the bridge. I can hear the clatter of cars rushing overhead. The sculpture is just as I remember it—the huge troll pushing up through the ground, his shiny hubcap eye, the real VW Beetle he's crushing in one of his giant hands.

My mom is nowhere in sight.

"She's behind the troll," I say.

"We need to wait for Mark and Nora," he says. "They'll be here in a few minutes."

But we don't have a few minutes. If she's not behind the troll, then it means she's taken off and we've lost her. "Do you have a flashlight?"

He sighs and turns on the flashlight app on his phone. "I'll check, okay? Just stay here," he says. He starts to slowly walk up the troll's arm. That's when I see something move out of the corner of my eye. Something that shouldn't be moving.

My stomach drops. "Spencer? Can a demon animate a nonliving thing?" Uncle Roy has never mentioned this, not once in all the time I've trained with him, so maybe my eyes are just playing tricks on me.

"I'm pretty sure that's just an urban legend," Spencer says. But as he walks up the troll's arm toward its shoulder, one of its long stone fingers begins to twitch.

"Not an urban legend," I say, my eyes widening.

The troll's shoulders start to roll, knocking Spencer off his feet. He scrambles on his hands and knees the rest of the way down the sculpture, crawling on all fours all the way over to me as the troll starts to hoist itself out of the ground.

I'm frozen to the spot as the troll's mouth opens like a gaping canyon, sending sand particles swirling through the air. It roars and its hubcap eye pops out. It pushes down on the VW Beetle as it tries to work itself free, and I hear the crunch of metal. The troll is only built from the waist up——there is no lower body to raise out of the ground——so how much damage can it really do?

The thought is barely in my head when the troll gives up on trying to stand up and lifts its long, long arms instead. Up toward the bridge. The bridge that hundreds of unsuspecting people are currently driving over.

"We have to get out of here," Spencer says, pulling me toward the street.

"We can't just leave! It's going to upend the bridge. There are people up there!"

Spencer shakes his head. "Shelby, this is dangerous," he says. "And we don't know what we're doing."

"Rule number one: Always work in pairs," I say. "There're two of us. We can handle it until the others get here. We have to."

Spencer glances at the troll, which is still roaring, its hands bracing against the steel beams of the bridge. He closes his eyes and takes a deep breath. "Okay, fine."

My hands are shaking as I hold my crucifix in front of me. Spencer stands beside me, his shoulder brushing mine.

"Deus, in nómine tuo salvum me fac—"

"Let God arise, and let His enemies be scattered—"

Our voices overlap, rising together.

"—and let them that hate Him flee from before His face—"

The troll roars with anger. It folds its fingers into a fist and then slams its fist into the ground a few feet from where we're standing, sending shockwaves through the earth. I reach for Spencer's hand.

"—as smoke vanishes, so let them vanish away—"

"—*et virtúte tua age causam meam*—"

I stop mid-incantation as my crucifix is suddenly ripped from my hands by some invisible force. The crucifix hovers in front of me just within reach, then bends in half and drops to the ground at my feet.

Spencer and I glance at each other. I'm beginning to wish I'd listened to him and waited for Mark and Nora when they come skidding up to us. They're out of breath from running.

Nora stands beside me and grabs my hand. The four of us form a line.

"As wax melts before the fire, so let the wicked perish at the presence of God!"

"*Nam supérbi insurréxerunt contra me, et violénti quæsiérunt vitam meam!*"

The troll begins to slow down, like it's trying to move through molasses—the combination of our incantations and the strength of our joined voices seem to be working.

As we continue to chant, the troll sinks slowly back down into the ground.

We keep chanting long after it finally stills. Just to be sure.

Spencer lets out a long breath. I can't stop shaking.

Did we do it?

I think we did it.

My mom appears from behind the troll. The sun has almost set, and her face is hidden by the shadows. My heart leaps and I want to run to her, but Spencer tightens his grip on my hand.

"Stop! Let me go," I say, trying to shake him off.

"Shelby, it could be a trick," Mark says. "We need to make sure the demon is really gone."

Nora puts her arm around me as Mark climbs cautiously up the hill toward my mom. He's holding his wooden cross in front of him. He gets a few feet from her when all of a sudden, just like my crucifix, he's lifted high into the air.

"Mark!" Spencer yells. This time he tries to run, and I clamp down on his hand.

Mark's own hands wrap around his throat. He squirms in the air, his legs kicking madly, as the demon makes him choke himself. His face is already turning purple and his eyes are beginning to bug out.

"Let God arise, and let His enemies be scattered!" Nora yells.

"*Deus, audi oratiónem meam; áuribus pércipe verba oris mei!*" I can feel tears coursing down my face. *Please, please let this work.*

My mom roars. Mark falls to the ground. He rolls onto his hands and knees, gasping for air.

We don't break the chain and we keep chanting, even as the sand around my mom starts to glow red. The ground beneath her shifts, and I'm terrified that a sinkhole is going to open and suck her under.

Suddenly, there's an ear-splitting sound of screaming. Beams of red light shoot toward the shifting sand. It's so hot, sweat is pouring off of me. It's like we're standing in the pit of hell. These red lights have to be all of the souls that came through the portal being sucked back into the underworld.

And then, as quickly as it started, the screaming stops. The red lights disappear. The sand stops moving, and the air around us cools by about a million degrees.

My mom crumples to the ground. Spencer lets go of my hand, and I'm vaguely aware of him sprinting to help Mark as I grab the holy water from my bag and run toward my mom.

Please, God, let her be okay.

I stand over her, and my breath hitches. She's lying on

her side, her dark hair covering her face. I don't think she's breathing.

I think she's dead.

My knees start to buckle. I'm on the edge of passing out when Nora rests a hand on my arm.

"It's okay, Shelby," she says calmly. "She's still breathing. And that's what I need you to do as well, okay? Just breathe." She helps me sit down on the ground, then takes the spray bottle from me and squirts some holy water on my mom's hand. Her skin doesn't react. "All clear," Nora says, and I crawl over to my mom.

I put her head in my lap, and she starts to stir. By the time her eyes flicker open and I see that they're back to their beautiful brown, I'm bawling.

"Shelby?" Her voice is weak. "What's happening?" She tries to sit up, but I gently push her back down.

"What's happening is that you're back," I say, my arms tightening around her. My body slumps with relief because the truth is, I really wasn't sure that this moment was ever going to happen. "I've got you back."

Chapter

26

I'M WAITING for Spencer in a dim corner of the library. Since neither of us had the chance to study for our history test yesterday amid all the chaos of saving my mom, he asked me to meet him here early this morning so we could cram before first period. I'm not sure how much good it will do at this point—besides not having studied, I'm exhausted from staying up most of the night. I didn't want to come to school today—I wanted to stay home with my mom—but Uncle

Roy insisted. He said it would be better to give her some space, let her catch her breath.

We've only had her back for a few hours, but I already know that my mom's not the same. She might never be the same. We have no idea what she lived through all these months; Uncle Roy says her memory might come back, but maybe it's best if it doesn't. Right now, it's enough that she's home.

The library doors *whoosh* open. Spencer walks in, and I sit up straighter. His dark hair is still damp from the shower and his white dress shirt is buttoned up wrong, like he put it on in the dark when he was still half-asleep. He's carrying two takeout cups of coffee. I'm suddenly glad that I listened to Uncle Roy and came to school.

"Hey," Spencer says, handing me one of the cups.

"Thanks."

He slides into the seat beside me. He's pale and has dark rings around his eyes, but I swear he's never looked so good. "How's your mom?"

I shrug. "She's all in one piece," I say. "Physically, anyway."

Spencer frowns, his dark eyes sparking with sympathy. "I'm sorry."

"Don't be. If it weren't for you and the others, we wouldn't even have her back." I take a small sip of coffee. "How's Mark?"

"His throat is pretty bruised and his voice is a bit raspy, but he'll be all right," he says.

A shiver runs through me as I remember how the demon made Mark choke himself, the way his face turned purple as he gasped for air, and how he dropped to the ground like a stone. If we hadn't managed to close the portal, it all would have ended very differently. My crucifix wouldn't have been the only thing that was ruined.

As if he knows what I'm thinking, Spencer leans over and pulls something from his bag. He clears his throat. "I, um . . . I made you this." He hands me a large silver cross adorned with different-size sapphire stones. "You should probably have Father Roy bless it before you use it."

Oh my God. He made me a bejeweled crucifix!

I run my finger over the Celtic protection symbol he's carved into the shiny silver on the back, along with my initials. It must have taken him all night to make this. But he did it. For me.

Spencer smiles nervously. "Do you like it?"

"Are you kidding? I love it," I say, hugging the crucifix to my chest. "It's perfect! Thank you."

His face relaxes. He stares at me for a moment and then he puts his arm on the back of my chair, his fingers brushing my shoulder. My heart is like thunder in my chest as he leans toward me and finally—*finally!*—kisses me.

Maybe it's the months of lead-up to this moment, all the waiting for something to happen, but this is not your average first kiss. There's nothing shy or reserved about it, no fumbling or awkwardness. This kiss is full of everything we haven't said to each other yet. It's way better than any emoji.

But as good as this kiss is—and it's *amazing*—it's just the first of many. This is our beginning. And from the way Spencer pulls me toward him like he can't get close enough, I know he feels the same way.

Chapter

27

PAINTING a ceiling is much harder than you'd think. My arms are already aching, and my mom and I have only covered about a quarter of my room, even though it feels like we've been at it for ages already.

My mom coughs. I glance over, worried that this activity is too much for her. Her hand is shaking as she dips the roller into the paint tray. She's only been back with us for a week, and she really should rest and get her strength back, but she insisted on helping me.

"Maybe we should take a break," I say, but she just shakes her head. Keeping busy seems to be her way of dealing with what happened to her. She doesn't have any memory of being possessed, and she keeps pressing us for details. Uncle Roy has reassured her that we'll tell her once she's recovered, but that's not a conversation either of us is looking forward to.

I hear a tap on my window. I have yet to replace the blinds Vanessa ripped down when she was destroying my room, so I can see her standing on the other side, holding up a pair of jeans.

I get down off the step stool and open the window, and she pulls herself through.

"You do know we have a perfectly good front door," I say.

"Which I can never come through again," she says, dusting herself off. "I can't face Father Roy."

Vanessa's eyes land on my mom. From the expression on her face, I can tell that she's shocked to see her. Not only because my mom's here—and not in Italy, as she was told—but because she's changed so much since the last time Vanessa saw her. The past months have been hard on my mom, and it's reflected in her graying hair and all the weight she's lost, in the haunted look in her eyes.

"Hi, Ms. Black," Vanessa says.

"Hi, Vanessa. Nice to see you again." Even my mom's voice is different. She doesn't say much, but when she does talk, she sounds much quieter.

Being possessed doesn't seem to have affected Vanessa in the same way. She says she's over it, but maybe that's because she was only under a demon's influence for a short time. My mom wants to talk to her about what happened to them both one day soon—she doesn't think Vanessa is as over it as she claims to be—but she's not quite ready yet.

As it turns out, I shouldn't have worried about Vanessa's reaction to learning that I'm an exorcist—she doesn't care. And I am super-relieved that I don't have to hide that part of myself from her anymore. I'm done with hiding who I am.

"You'll have to face Uncle Roy eventually," I say, hoping that her fear of Uncle Roy is enough to distract her from asking my mom questions about Italy.

"I fractured his elbow!" she says.

"He's not going to tell anyone that you did it."

"But *I* know that I did it." She hands me a castoff pair of jeans, her favorite pair, to replace the jeans of mine that she tore. "I think these should fit you."

There's no way they'll fit me—Vanessa is three inches shorter than me—but I appreciate the gesture.

She takes in the paintbrush in my hand, then looks upward. "Um, why are you guys painting the ceiling?"

"This color keeps evil spirits out," I say.

"Huh," she says. "I guess we're going to have to do my room next, then."

Like my mom, Vanessa doesn't have much memory of when she was possessed. And like my mom, I haven't told her much. I'm not sure she really wants to hear that she levitated up to the ceiling she's about to help paint.

I hand her a paint roller. "I'll help you with your room if you promise me that you aren't going to fool around with Ouija boards anymore."

"Trust me, I am done with Ouija boards." She slides the roller through the paint tray.

"What's this about Ouija boards?" Uncle Roy pokes his head in the door. "Oh, hi, Vanessa," he says. "I didn't hear you come in."

Vanessa squeaks in response, too embarrassed to even look his way.

"Haint blue?" he says, glancing up at the ceiling and snorting. "Old wives' tale."

A shadow of a smile crosses my mom's lips. "Like your flower paintings?" It's the first time she's made any attempt at humor since we got her back, and it gives me hope. Maybe it won't be long before she's back to her old self.

Uncle Roy purses his lips. "Yes, well, that's just proof that it's all balderdash," he says. "Those paintings did us no good. Vanessa was able to get in rather easily."

Vanessa's face is burning.

"But I invited her in," I say. "The protection doesn't work if you invite an evil spirit in."

"You're thinking of vampires, not demons," Uncle Roy responds, sighing. He shakes his head, then turns to my mom. "Robin, would you help me with a report when you have a moment?" he asks. He gestures to his right arm, encased in a sling, to remind us that he can't write his report himself.

I know this is Uncle Roy's way of trying to get her involved. He hasn't given up hope that my mom will be his partner again, even though she says she's done with exorcisms. She wasn't happy when she learned that he's been training me, but I'm hoping to convince her to let me continue studying with Uncle Roy once he's recovered. The portal's been closed, but that doesn't mean that our work is done—there will always be demons. But hopefully now there will be less of them.

"Yes, of course," she says. She sets her paintbrush down and wipes her hands on an old T-shirt we're using as a paint rag. "You girls okay to finish up?"

"We've got it covered."

She gives me a quick hug. She hasn't stopped hugging me

since she got home. And I'm more than happy to let her. We have a lot of time to make up for.

"You know, this isn't as nearly as fun as it looks," Vanessa says a few minutes later. She runs a hand across her forehead, smearing a blob of paint on her skin.

"I never said it would be fun." I stretch to reach the corner of my ceiling. Maybe this is just a silly superstition—maybe it's crazy to believe that a coat of blue paint will keep me from harm—but it makes me feel better.

Vanessa grimaces, but she doesn't give up. She keeps painting, even though I know she's hating every second of it. But we make the best of it, talking and laughing and complaining about how much our arms ache, until eventually we finish. And as I climb down from the step stool, I realize that this moment has already become one of our stories, one that we'll tell over and over until it's as worn as an old dollar bill.

Epilogue

Case Number: EX104-17-3856

Incident: The Exorcism of Mrs. Florence Merriweather

Exorcist: Shelby Black

June 18, 1600 hours. Zelda Horvath, one of our elderly parishioners, came by the rectory this morning to ask for help exorcising her friend, Mrs. Florence Merriweather. As Father Roy claims his elbow is still not fully healed, he

asked me to accompany Mrs. Horvath
to her home and attend to
Mrs. Merriweather's exorcism by
myself.

Father Roy's elbow only seems to bother
him when he's trying to get out of doing
something, so naturally I was suspicious.
Especially because the only other time
he's sent me out on my own was when
he wanted me to exorcise a person who
was not even possessed (see the
"exorcism" of Shane Harris). Also, he
was trying not to smile when he asked
me to take care of it.

And it turns out that I was right to be
suspicious of his motives! Because
when we arrived at Mrs. Horvath's
apartment and she opened the door, I
caught my first glimpse of Mrs. Florence
Merriweather dragging her butt
across the beige carpet. Right then,
I knew for sure that I had been
tricked.

Yes. Mrs. Merriweather is a <u>dog</u>. A toy poodle, to be specific. Tiny and gray and fluffy, with purple bows on her ears. Cute until she tries to sink her teeth into your ankle, which she attempted to do to me as soon as I walked through the door.

I did not even know it was possible for pets to be possessed, since Father Roy has never once shared this information with me. I wasn't sure the regular methods of exorcising a demon would work on an animal, but since I had nothing else to go on, I pulled out my crucifix and holy water. I figured that it would be an easy-enough task—I mean, expelling a demon from a dog has to be easier than exorcising a human, right?—and it might have been if Mrs. Horvath hadn't been yelling at me every two seconds not to harm her precious baby.

"Almost done?" Spencer asks.

I glance over at him. He's sitting behind Uncle Roy's

desk, repeatedly tossing a yellow smiley-face stress ball in the air, waiting for me to finish this stupid report for Uncle Roy. Spencer's a major distraction with his sexy dark hair and perfectly sculpted arms. He's rolled the cuffs of his shirt up to his elbows to give me a good glimpse, probably because he's bored of waiting and knows his arms are my kryptonite.

"Just about." I quickly scribble the rest of the details.

> Said the incantation as
> Mrs. Merriweather alternated between
> snapping at my ankles and floating
> through the air like a helium balloon.
> Gave her a good squirt of holy water,
> right in the ear. She yelped and ran
> behind the couch, but I think that's
> because she was scared of the water and
> not because her skin was on fire. I'm
> 85-percent sure that the exorcism worked.

I sign my name at the bottom of the paper and get up to toss the report onto Uncle Roy's desk. Spencer leans back in the leather chair as I approach. I'm about to slide into his lap when Uncle Roy comes into the office.

"Mr. Callaghan," he says. He makes a shooing gesture, and Spencer gives him a sheepish smile as he stands up and slides past him. Uncle Roy sits down in his chair, his eyes narrowing as he notices that Spencer's been messing with his stuff.

I grab my bag. We'd best be getting out of here before he blows. Spencer and I are halfway out the door—so close, I'm almost home free—when Uncle Roy says, "Oh, Shelby? Don't forget—"

"We have training in an hour." I roll my eyes. "I know."

He gives me a small smile and folds his hands together. "Actually, why don't you take the afternoon off?"

"Thanks," I say, smiling back at him. Maybe it's because he knows I've been working really hard lately—both at school and at my exorcism studies. Or maybe this is his way of making up for the fact that he sent me to exorcise a dog. Whatever his reasons, I'm happy to skip training for the day and spend time with my boyfriend.

I duck out of the office before Uncle Roy changes his mind. Spencer's leaning against the wall. I reach for his hand, threading my fingers through his, and we walk down the hall together, leaving all thoughts of Uncle Roy—and demons— behind us.

At least for the moment.

Acknowledgments

Being a published author is something I've dreamed about since I was eight years old. This is my second book, but it all still feels like a dream.

Endless gratitude to my amazing editor, Kat Brzozowski, for her enthusiasm, spot-on insight, and guidance. Thank you, Jean Feiwel, Lauren Scobell, Emily Settle, Hayley Jozwiak, Kayla Overbey, Mandy Veloso, Samantha Hoback, Rachel Diebel, Amanda Mustafic, and Liz Dresner, and all the rest of the wonderful Swoon Reads team. Working with all of you is such a joy.

Thank you to Jessica Hansen for providing the perfect title for this book.

Thank you to the team at Raincoast Books, especially Fernanda Viveiros and Melissa Pellegrin, and to all the bloggers and readers who supported *Wesley James Ruined My Life*.

I'm lucky to be surrounded by so many talented and generous writers, all of whom I've turned to many times for advice and support: Eric Brown, Rebecca Christiansen, Sandy Hall, Abby Wener Herlin, Michelle Krys, Ruth Lauren, Maggie Martin, Tiana Smith, and Katy Upperman.

I have the greatest cheering section an author could ever ask for. Thank you: Corey Allen, Dallas and Todd Depagie, Harpreet Gill, Niki Glenning, Leiko Greaves, Brian and Joy Honeybourn, Barbara Hsiao, Kate Hunter, Mandy James, Elizabeth Koprich, Cyprien Lomas, Tracey Lundell, Shaun and Carianne McKay, Jennifer McKenzie, Caely-Ann McNabb, Pam Morrison, Linda Ong, Stacie Palivos, Karam and Varinder Rai, Nadine Silver, Jim and Jela Stanic, Robert Stanic, Ange Grim, and Anna Tennick.

And thank you to my husband, Tony, for his endless support, love, and encouragement—I wouldn't be here without you. And our daughter, Lila, my other dream come true.